# VAMPIRE SIRE

*(Red Rider: Part 1)*

////

# J.R. RAIN

# THE VAMPIRE FOR HIRE SERIES

Moon Dance
Vampire Moon
American Vampire
Moon Child
Christmas Moon (novella)
Vampire Dawn
Vampire Games
Moon Island
Moon River
Vampire Sun
Moon Dragon
Moon Shadow
Vampire Fire
Midnight Moon
Moon Angel
Vampire Sire
Moon Master
Dead Moon
Moon World

Published by
Crop Circle Books
212 Third Crater, Moon

Copyright © 2018 by J.R. Rain

All rights reserved.

Printed in the United States of America.

ISBN: 9781718081048

## *Dedication*

To Diwamani. He laughs a lot, reads my books, and sports a robust beard. Everything I look for in a friend.

VAMPIRE SIRE

# 1.

I was folding laundry and watching Judge Judy when I came across Anthony's latest masterpiece.

At first glance, it looked like any other pair of tighty-whities. Upon second glance, it was obvious there was something very, very wrong here. For instance, that wasn't a shadow I was seeing.

Nope, just nope.

Nope, nope, nope.

I had fought wolf men, demons and even the devil himself, but none gave me more pause than the rolled-up abomination tucked in the far corner of the laundry basket.

"Lord, give me strength," I said, wondering idly if my prayers fell on deaf ears. And if they did, well, screw it. I'd answer my own damn prayers.

Truth be told, while loading from washer to

dryer, I suspected there had been something amiss: a strange, dark swath seen in my peripheral vision. But I ignored it, hoping like crazy that what I was seeing had been my imagination. That maybe, just maybe, my washer was haunted by a shadow man.

But there was no denying *this*.

*This* was epic. *This* made me question my parenting skills. Obviously, something, somewhere had gone off the rails somewhere. A disconnect. Somehow, the proper use of toilet paper must have fallen on deaf ears... or through the butt cracks.

I sighed, said another prayer... and reached for That Which Should Not Exist.

But it did. And it was in my laundry basket.

"Lord, help me."

\*\*\*

Judge Judy was on point, as usual.

Her ability to size up someone was uncanny. In fact, it was positively supernatural. At present, some punk was trying to convince her that he wasn't stoned, and that he wasn't responsible for a loan his friend had given him. Except, of course, he kept laughing, and talked way too much, and his eyelids might have been mostly closed... or made of lead. Judge Judy even cracked a smile, which always makes me smile. In the end, the stoner lost but didn't seem to care that he lost—in his exit interview, he asked where the closest Taco Bell was.

VAMPIRE SIRE

With Anthony's underwear now in the "burn" pile, and Judge Judy just signing off, a car pulled up outside my house, a car I had been expecting. Through the mostly closed window shades, I watched the driver try to figure out the angles of the cul-de-sac curb, then watched as she gave up and basically parked with her car's ass sticking way out into the cul-de-sac. Then I watched her get out, straighten her skirt, brush back her hair, and head up the driveway toward the gate in the chain-link fence. It's a short gate, but she fumbled with it a few times, pushed it the wrong way, then pulled it the right way, then stepped through. She collected herself again, took a deep breath or two, and headed along the short path to my front door.

I pulled it open before she could knock. "Lauren Skinner?" I asked.

"Samantha Moon?"

"Boy, we're good at this game," I said. "Come in."

She did and I showed her to my back office with its bookcase and sliding glass door. Little did she know that an angel had once appeared to me here, or that ghosts sometimes materialized in the very same chair where she was now sitting. Or that a vampire was sitting across from her now. Or that, just a few months ago, I'd killed the devil himself. No, I'm not crazy. At least, I don't think I am.

"Cute office," she said.

"Thank you."

"You work from home?" she asked.

"I do."

"As a private eye?"

I nodded. "And an international woman of mystery."

She laughed sharply at that. "I'm not even sure what that means."

"It's from a Mike Myers movie."

"I see."

"You never saw it."

"No." Pause. "I told you who I work for on the phone, correct?"

"A probate attorney."

She nodded. "Michael Lansky, to be exact."

Of course, the moment she had mentioned the name over the phone, I had researched the man and confirmed he was legit enough to at least meet with her, his assistant.

"Are you an attorney, too?" I asked.

"Not quite. I am his lead researcher... or fact-gatherer."

She handed me a card: *Alaine Juni, Researcher*

"In essence, I unofficially act as the executrix for our distinguished clients."

"Distinguished in what way? And is that the feminine for executor?"

"Yes. And as far as what way, we will get to that, Ms. Moon, I promise. I'm not trying to be coy, but I do need some information first."

"Sure," I said.

I liked her, so I was willing to wait. Interestingly, although I could read her mind, it was... well, impenetrable. In fact, a song was looping in the foreground of her thoughts, a song that I found nearly impossible to push through. I probably could if I tried hard enough, but I didn't want to or need to. At least not now, not with the promise of more information later. I studied her again and saw her aura plain enough. A sure indicator that she was definitely mortal.

"About six years ago, our client was killed. He left behind a very large estate."

"And you are telling me this, why?"

"Because you are named in his will."

I mentally went back in time six years. Not a good time in my life, admittedly. Danny had just left me. I had found myself living in a hotel. Of course, during that time period, I had also flown for the first time, too. What else had happened six years ago? Hmm. I plumbed my memory. I might have superhuman strength and teleport around the world—and even off-world—but I didn't have a super memory. Let's see. Well, I had been shot by Rand the vampire hunter six years ago. I had met Kingsley six years ago, too. Oh, and I had met Sherbet six years ago. I drummed my fingers, my nails clacking away, thinking hard. I had been given the first of a series of medallions six years ago. The ruby medallion, in fact. A medallion worn by my attacker. An attacker who had been killed by the same hunter who had shot me. Lots was going on, six years ago.

"Go on," I said.

"You never formally met my client, but you did, in fact, meet."

We were talking about my attacker. I was sure of it. So I said nothing, reliving those terrible few minutes on a trail at Hillcrest Park in Fullerton, a few minutes that would forever—and I mean *forever*—change my life.

I felt my jaw clenching. "Go on."

"Like I said, you never formally met him, but he knew of you. In fact, he knew a great deal about you."

My mostly dormant heart kicked in, and I could feel it thudding dully in my chest. Sometimes, I wondered if the whole purpose of my heart was to help me gauge my emotions. Well, it was beating now, and for good reasons. A very scary time in my life was playing out in my head, from my attack on the trail, to waking up in the hospital, to the confusion that followed. So. Much. Confusion.

"What's his name?" I heard myself ask.

"Jeffcock Letholdus."

I said nothing. Not at first. Then I asked her to repeat it, and she did. I asked her to repeat it again. She did, again.

"You are saying Jeff*cock*, correct?" I asked.

"I am, yes."

"And that's a name people give their actual

kids?"

"Not so much now, no. But in the Middle Ages, yes."

"The Middle Ages?"

"Yes, Ms. Moon."

I drummed my nails on my desk and caught Alaine watching me drum my nails. I nearly snatched my hands away and hid them in my lap, as was my custom. Instead, I left them there—along with my ghoulishly misshapen nails. Hands someone would see on, say, a horror poster. Hands and nails and fingers of something that might snatch one's ankles from under the bed. The sort of claws that left deep and bloody furrows in their victims. These weren't nice hands, and these certainly weren't nice nails.

Still, I drummed them slowly, noting again the thickness and sharpness of the nails. And maybe for the first time, I also noticed their purpose: to strike fear in the hearts of man. Except the woman before me—the woman with the looping song in her thoughts—wasn't afraid. No, not at all.

"I think we both know to whom we are referring, Ms. Moon," she finally said, her gaze sliding up from the desktop and deep enough into my eyes that I wondered if she also saw the flames that existed therein. I had it on good authority that such flames represented Elizabeth herself, the dark master who possessed me. "And I think we both know what he did to you twelve years ago."

"And what did he do to me twelve years ago?" I asked.

For some reason, I wanted to hear it from her. No, I *needed* to hear it from her. Hearing it from her would be the confirmation I needed that the events on that fateful night so long ago were, in fact, real. That I hadn't made them up, or filled in the gaps. That, in fact, they had happened as I remembered them happening. Not that I ever questioned my own version of the story, but all I'd had was my memory... and that was it. My memory, and the resulting aftereffects, of course. Never before had anyone corroborated my version. Indeed, who could? Just me... and my attacker. And now, amazingly, this woman. This stranger.

There went my heart again, beat-beat-beating in my chest.

"You were attacked twelve years ago, Sam. You were attacked ruthlessly, deliberately, and with reckless abandon. You were left to die, but you wouldn't die, of course. You would do the exact opposite. Live forever. Twelve years ago, my client—now deceased—rendered you into a vampire, and your life has never been the same since."

## 2.

"No one likes a know-it-all," I said.

"I don't know it all, Ms. Moon. But I know enough."

"Since when do vampires make wills and retain attorneys?" I asked. I felt oddly deflated. This wasn't the closure I'd been looking for. No, not by a long shot.

"Many do, Sam. May I call you Sam?"

"Knock yourself out."

"My employer is sympathetic, shall we say, to the undead."

"Your employer is a vampire?" I asked.

"Werewolf."

I nodded. For some reason, The Hairy Ones seemed to gravitate toward the practice of law.

"My employer helps those like you navigate the

world of mortals. After all, special care must be considered if one is immortal... or close to it. Not all immortals run through graveyards and aimlessly stalk city streets at night. Like you, some have families. Many own extensive properties. And many fake their deaths to properly bequeath such estates to those they love or care about. As you know—and someday will discover firsthand—supernaturals such as yourself will outlive loved ones and friends. Sometimes, they will outlive governments and whole countries. An astute attorney can help a vampire or were creature start over again."

"But that's not what happened here," I said. "Jeffdick—"

"Jeffcock."

"Same thing, did *not* fake his death."

"No, Sam. He was killed. By the very same hunter who attacked you."

"And you know this, how?"

She smiled warmly at me... and a little knowingly, too. Her lip quirked up and it hit me. I had seen that same expression on my daughter.

"Yes, Sam. I am a telepath. A particularly strong one. No, not as strong as your daughter, but I, too, can dip into the minds of immortals."

"So there are no secrets from you?"

"No, not really."

"And you effectively block your own thoughts with the looping song."

"I do, Sam."

"Fine. Whatever. Then you know all about me."

"Not all, Sam. Unlike you or your daughter, I can only catch flashes of the strongest hits across the prefrontal cortex. I can't dip further than that."

"But you are mortal."

"Yes. You are wondering how I developed such abilities."

"Lucky guess," I said.

"Not so lucky. Oh, I see you are joking. You could probably surmise how such abilities develop in humans."

I could, actually. My daughter's own abilities were due to her close proximity to me, and, in particular, the power level of the entity possessing me. Turned out, Elizabeth was one helluva powerful bee-atch.

"Yes, Sam. You are correct. Turns out, my boss is pretty damn powerful too. One of the most powerful of shifters. And yes, he is friends with Kingsley Fulcrum."

"Small world," I said.

"Indeed."

"Now get the fuck out of my head," I said, and threw up the most powerful barrier I could, one that had been taught to me by my daughter herself, one that caused enough interference to sometimes give even her fits.

"Very well, Sam," she said, blinking. "Now, shall we get down to business?"

I knew she was here for business. I also knew

she was here because I had been included in someone's will. What I hadn't known was that certain someone just so happened to be the very same bastard who had attacked and turned me. Admittedly, a number of thoughts raced through my mind. Admittedly, they all took a backseat to one: *curiosity*.

"Okay," I said. "Fire away."

She nodded, reached into her briefcase somewhere by her feet but below my eyeline. She withdrew a few sheets of paper and laid them on the desk before me. "First off, Mr. Letholdus has left you a sizable inheritance."

"Sizable in what way?"

"He left you his home in the Fullerton Hills, including everything within and everything below."

"Below?"

"Mr. Letholdus had... exquisite tastes, you could say. He is leaving you his collection to do with as you wish."

"In his basement?"

"Not quite a basement, but close."

"And you know what's in this basement?"

"I do, yes."

"And you won't tell me?"

"No."

"I have ways of making you tell me," I said.

"I know, Sam. I'm hoping none of this results in violence. I am, of course, outfitted in silver, and have on my person a number of weapons, including a silver-tinged spray that you wouldn't like at all."

"Fair enough. But for the record, I was talking about tickling."

"Of course you were. Shall we continue?"

"Please do."

"The home itself would be considered, by all accounts, a mansion. It occupies its own hillock on the outskirts of Fullerton. Its views are impressive, as is its construction and general layout. Truly, it is one of my favorite buildings in Orange County, and I am not shy about expressing some jealousy. Then again, if anyone is more deserving of the home, it would be you, one of his victims."

"You spoke to him?"

She nodded. "Often, especially after your attack."

"He spoke of my attack?"

"Not directly, but he hinted at it, and the firm was aware of it, based on the updates to his will."

I nodded, momentarily at a loss as to what to ask next.

"Additionally, he mentioned that he was certain he was being hunted by a clever foe, someone who, up to that point, he was unable to pinpoint. He was careful to make sure his will was finalized, and he was careful to include you in it."

The hunter would have been Rand. And Jeffcock had a reason to be concerned. After all, Rand had finished the job, killing the old vampire... and then coming for me next. Last I checked, I hadn't been killed, and had somehow made it through, thanks to a carefully timed turn of my shoulder, which still sometimes ached, even years later. Silver was a bitch to my kind.

"What did he look like?"

"Mr. Letholdus?"

"Yes."

"For a vampire, he looked elderly."

"How many vampires have you seen?"

"Dozens, Sam. But Jeffcock was one of the oldest-looking. Clearly, he had been turned later in life."

"And when would that have been?"

"He let it be known that he'd been hanging around since the 1600s. We knew him to be one of the oldest vampires—and not just in physical appearance—in the world."

"How long had he been in Fullerton?"

"Nearly two decades. Well, nineteen years."

I thought about that. By now, I, too, had been in Fullerton for almost two decades from the time when Danny and I had settled in, gotten jobs and started our family. Curiouser and curiouser.

"He lived alone?"

"I only knew of him during his last few years. But he lived with servants. Both of whom still maintain the property."

I snapped my fingers. A question that had been nagging at me sprang to the forefront of my thoughts. "Why now? It's been, what, six years since his death?"

She nodded at that. "Exactly six years. I think, perhaps, it's better to show you why. We have a standardized agreement in all of our contracts with all of our clients."

She spun the paper around and pointed to a numbered clause, written in tiny print. Luckily, my eyes are perfect. In a nutshell, it stated that the inheritance would remain in probate until a period of six years had passed.

I sat back, satisfied but still curious. "Why six years?"

"It's a standard clause for our... eternal clients."

"But why?"

"My boss, the author of the clause, had learned over his very long career that immortals are wont to have a change of heart and/or mysteriously return from the grave. Six years seems to be the ideal buffer or grace period. It is safe to assume that, considering the circumstances of Mr. Letholdus' death, he won't be coming back any time soon."

"You know this how?"

"I saw the body, Ms. Moon," she said. "He had been thoroughly vanquished by both silver-tipped arrow and, shortly after, by fire."

"Any chance it wasn't him?" I asked.

"We had a DNA sample from him, a standard requirement. As you might have guessed, his murder was not reported to the authorities."

"Was he buried?"

"No. He was burned further in the crematorium under his home."

*A crematorium under his home?* "Then why wait the requisite six years?"

"Because our contracts are upheld to the letter... and with immortals, anything can happen. My employer claims he has seen it all. Six years seems to be a safe waiting period."

"To truly confirm the immortal is dead and gone?"

"In blunt terms, yes."

"So what now?" I asked.

She reached into her briefcase again and pulled out two more pieces of paper. She pushed the first document toward me. "This is a transfer-on-death deed, Ms. Moon. As you can see, Mr. Letholdus took the time to make the process of transfer as seamless as possible."

I nodded dumbly as the reality of this situation began to set in. My mind was both empty and racing. Like a prop gun firing off blanks.

"And here is the latest assessment of the house," she said, pushing the second piece of paper at me.

The house, I couldn't help but notice, was valued at $5.7 million.

"Is this really happening?" I asked.

"Yes, Sam, it's happening. You need only to sign the deed of transfer and the house is all yours."

"But I'm not entirely sure *why* this is happening."

"Mr. Letholdus predicted your confusion, which is why he left you a personal note. You'll see that within the note, there are a series of instructions for you, personally, instructions that I cannot help you with, nor can anyone."

I opened my mouth to speak again, but nothing came out, although I might have hissed a little like a flat tire. Or a snake. I closed my mouth again.

"Your confusion is understandable, which is why he left you the note. But I will add this: Mr. Letholdus wasn't like the others of your kind."

"My kind?" I asked.

"Do we need to dance around the subject, Ms. Moon? I have seen your memories. And I see your nails. I also noted you cast no reflection in the glass of the framed pictures hanging in your hallway. You are a vampire, through and through."

"Fine. Go on."

"Very well. As mentioned, I have come across many others of your kind, and I have seen inside the minds of all. Trust me when I say this, Ms. Moon, you would not believe what I have found inside the minds of other vampires. I have seen what they do to those they feed on, not all of whom they kill. I have seen the grotesque arrangements some vampires force upon their mortal victims. I have seen the lives stolen and the pain inflicted. Mercifully, my own telepathy is limited, and I cannot go deep enough, but I have seen enough to haunt me for the rest of my days."

"Yet, still you do your job."

She held up her hands. "I am afraid I am in this for life. Little did I know what I was signing on for when I first took the position. My own employer is not without his own sins."

"He feeds from you."

"But of course, Sam." She paused, looked away, and the song inside her head faltered enough for me to see in her mind, see her holding her wrists out, while a very, very large man hovered next to her, hungrily feeding from them. I looked at the very same wrists and noted they were as smooth as can be. No sign of scarring, which was to be expected. The bite of an immortal always heals cleanly. Perhaps it is necessary to cover their attacks; after all, not all victims recall being attacked, and that is certainly for the best.

"A werewolf who feeds on blood?" I asked.

"He is... a half-breed, Sam. Ah, I see this is a new concept for you."

It was and it wasn't. I'd heard about such half-breeds during my time in New Orleans and, well, all the way back to the Civil... but that was a story for another time and place.

"My employer can be nourished by either flesh or blood."

"You want me to kick his ass?"

She smiled sadly. "No, Sam. It is an arrangement I... enjoy."

I nodded, understanding the close bond between

a vampire and a consenting feeder. "It makes you stronger."

"Yes, Sam. My own telepathy and fledgling telekinesis grows with each feeding. Telekinesis? I didn't know I had it in me."

"You're a big girl, so I won't mention how dangerous this arrangement could be to your health."

"I understand the risks, Sam. And I welcome them."

"Very well. You were saying?"

She nodded. "Mr. Letholdus was not like the others. Like you, he drank from animals."

"Unlike me, he kept slaves."

"Servants only, Sam. And they came with the house."

"Fine," I said.

"You will soon come to realize that your attacker—the vampire who rendered you into what you are today—meant you no harm."

"Pshaw," I said dismissively. "I beg to differ."

She pushed on. "You will note, Sam, that greater powers than he orchestrated your attack. I assure you, he was most displeased."

"Seemed happy enough."

"There is more to the story, Sam. But perhaps you should hear it from him. But just know that our client was not in the habit of turning other vampires. In fact, you were his first and only. He will explain the significance of that in his letter."

"Significance of what?" I asked.

"His connection to you."

"I don't even know what that means."

"Truthfully, Sam? I don't either. But he will explain it more in his letter. From there, what happens next is up to you."

I waved her words away. "Fine. Whatever. The vampire who threw me a few dozen feet into a tree and virtually tore my throat out is a saint. What's your point?"

"There is more to the story, or so he hinted."

"You do not know the story?"

"No, Sam. Just know that he was not like the others. He kept to himself, kept to his pursuits."

"What pursuits?"

"You will learn soon enough. He was a quiet man, often disappearing for months at a time."

"Let me guess... his pursuits?"

"I would imagine so, yes. His neighbors, undoubtedly, would never have guessed his true nature. He kept the monster within him in check. Mostly."

"Mostly?"

"You will see soon enough, Sam. Now, will you be signing the deed?"

"What happens when I do?"

"You will be the sole owner of his home and—"

"And everything within."

"Yes, Sam."

I stared at the paper, and the little yellow arrow

tabs that were pointed at the various lines where I needed to sign. The tabs looked... absurd. That vampires played by human rules suddenly seemed absurd, too. That the vampire who had attacked me had also left me his very home was, perhaps, the most absurd of all. On principle, I should have refused the inheritance. I should have torn up the document and ordered Ms. Alaine out. But I didn't. After all, hadn't Jeffcock left me with another kind of inheritance, too? Hadn't I inherited, in a way, his own tainted blood? His vampiric legacy? Wasn't giving me a house the least he could do?

I took in some air, held it, and then forgot I was holding it. Finally, I said, "I can sell this house, no?"

"You can do anything you want with it," she said. "But might I offer a suggestion?"

"Offer away."

"You might want to give it a thorough inspection."

"I'll be sure to do that."

"Please do," she said, and handed me her pen.

I paused only briefly before accepting it and, with my head spinning and my hand (perhaps the first time in years) shaking, I signed my name to the deed.

# 3.

"You're kidding?"

"I'm not kidding."

"C'mon, Sam. This is a joke, right? A mansion?"

"No joke and, yes, a mansion. I think."

"You haven't seen it yet?"

"No, Allison," I said. "That's why I'm calling you. Get your butt down here ASAP and help me check it out."

"Sam, I have clients."

"Ditch them."

"I can't just ditch them."

"Yes, you can."

"No, I can't, Sam. This is how I pay my bills."

"Ditch them and help me explore a creepy old mansion."

"How creepy?"

"Put it this way... there are still two people working there."

"How long has he been dead?"

"Six years, give or take a few months."

"Who pays them?"

"No idea."

"And your attacker's name really is Jeffcock?"

"It is."

"Sam, are you bull—"

"I'm not bullshitting you. This is real. This is happening, and I need your ass out here."

"You do?"

"Yes, dammit."

"Sam..."

"Look, I'm going in two hours, enough time to get your booty here."

"I really shouldn't."

"You shouldn't, but you will."

I heard the sound of fingernails drumming on her end of the line.

"Fine, Sam. Fine. But I'll probably lose this client."

"Isn't he the middle-aged guy who's always trying to look down your top?"

"Yeah, how did you—"

"Because all your middle-aged clients try to look down your top. Hell, I try to look down your top. Now get your butt over here and help me explore this damn freaky house. Oh, and bring me a vanilla latte from Starbucks."

"Anything else?"

"A scone."

"Fine, see you soon."

"And Allison?"

"Yeah?"

"Love you."

"You're incorrigible, Sam."

"I'm waiting..."

"Fine. Love you, too."

I grinned, and clicked off.

\*\*\*

With Starbucks cup in hand, and the scone already devoured, I sat in the passenger seat while Allison navigated through the Fullerton Hills in her old Camry.

"You could have at least driven, Sam."

"I could have."

"Sometimes, I think you take advantage of me."

"Just sometimes?"

"Bitch."

I grinned. "Turn left here."

"Like it's some great honor being your friend or something."

"I never said that."

"Well, *you* should be honored being *my* friend."

"I am," I said.

"Do you really mean that?"

"Sure," I said.

"That didn't sound too convincing, Sam."

I put my hand on her shoulder. "Allison Lopez, you're the baddest ass-est witch I have ever known, and it is my great honor to be your friend."

"I'm the *only* witch you know."

"True. But you're still kinda badass."

"I am, aren't I?"

I grinned, glanced at the directions on my phone and pointed toward another street. It wasn't much of a street at all. That Google Maps knew of it at all was further evidence of their all-encompassing invasion into our lives.

"There's a street there?" asked Allison.

"According to Google Maps. And Google Maps knows all, sees all."

"You're weird, Sam."

"You can say that again, but don't. Turn there."

She shrugged and turned up what appeared to be an overgrown utility road at the far end of a mostly empty, winding street. The heavily weeded path showed little, if any, sign of use in the past decade. Or, in this case, in the past six years. As we bounced along, a view of much of Fullerton opened up to us below. If I had to guess, I would say we were at the highest point in Fullerton, which wasn't saying much when compared to other high points around the state, but for Fullerton, it was impressive enough. Wooded valleys filled with stunted, twisted oaks, dropped away. Homes seemingly stacked on top of each other crowded the adjacent hill, but the stacking part could have just been a perspective issue. I smelled skunk, and a number of squirrels and rabbits dashed out of the Camry's path. Shadows fell over the road and soon, we found ourselves in an overgrown living tunnel of greenery. Poor Allison's car pushed bravely through the brambles, but the thorns and broken branches did a number on her paint.

At one point, when something sharp and nasty was really grinding into her paint job, she looked at me, nostrils flared. "Really, Sam?"

"Just keep going."

"My car..."

"We'll buff it out later."

"I hate you."

"No, you don't."

"Yes, I do. I'm already the only one driving a Camry in Beverly Hills, Sam. Like, the *only* one. How's it going to look when I'm driving a scratched-up Camry, to boot?"

"Like a woman who isn't consumed by materialism?"

"Grrr."

"Keep going."

She did, and soon, we were in a clearing... and what a clearing it was. A beautiful, manicured garden as big as a football field spread before us in all directions. I counted not one, but five bubbling fountains, scattered over the grass. Two of the fountains sported bosomy sea nymphs. Or mermaids. I wasn't sure of the difference. One had a tail. Or a fluke, or whatever the hell they were called. Recently, I'd heard Kingsley talking in his sleep about a mermaid. And not just talking, but emoting what I thought was real emotion. Then again, he'd been talking into his pulverized pillow and I couldn't make out much. Still, I'd asked him about Alexis the next morning—a name he'd moaned enough—and he only mumbled something unintelligible and went back to sleep. Kingsley didn't talk much about his past, and what little I'd managed to learn, I'd had to work hard for. And I was gonna have to work for information on Alexis. But it would be worth it. A mermaid? Seriously?

Anyway, beyond the vast expanse of grass was a house to rival Kingsley's own estate, except this one was older and sported Corinthian columns holding up a wide veranda, and an epic, sweeping, wraparound porch that had probably seen its share of lemonades and rocking chairs on summer days. That is, until a vampire came to town.

Now the deck was empty of any furniture, rocking or otherwise. Not even a wicker stool. As we continued along a crushed seashell drive, I could see now that my eyes weren't playing tricks on me. Great swaths of paint had long since peeled away, exposing graying, old wood beneath. One of the supporting columns had a deep crack that ran up the middle of it, and the porch itself was leaning and probably not up to code. The roof was sagging, too, and the whole place, unless my eyes were playing a trick on me, seemed to lean to the right.

"You inherited this?"

"Er, yes."

"Can you get a refund?"

"I don't think that's how it works."

"Were you aware that you were inheriting the setting for, like, every horror movie ever?"

"I was not aware of it, but I am now."

The closer we got, the more dilapidated the place seemed. If the paint hadn't already peeled off, it was in the process of peeling. The exposed clapboard siding, which usually ran in parallel intervals, wasn't always running in parallel intervals. Some of the pieces were hanging free. Others were missing altogether. Most were warped and bowed.

Speaking of warped, the wraparound porch looked like a rolling, gray sea, minus the foam and wind... and mermaids. From here, I could see gaping holes in the porch where the planks were gone. I was beginning to think I knew where the skunks were living. Allison parked in front of the "stairs."

"Sam, this place isn't safe."

"Don't judge a book by its cover."

"Unless the book doesn't have a cover."

I looked at Allison. She smirked.

"You're proud of that one, aren't you?" I asked.

She shrugged a little, leaning down and looking

up at the house through the windshield. "Kinda."

I looked up, too, and was certain I spotted a shadow shift from a window on the upper floor. "Maybe I could turn it into an Airbnb."

"For vampires?"

"And other freaks." I produced a set of antique keys from my pocket. "C'mon, let's check out the inside."

"Do we have to?"

"There are two people still living here," I said. "I need to check on them."

"Well, they've gotten along fine all these years without you."

"Maybe. I'll see for myself. Now, come on."

Speaking of covers, Allison was right about one thing: the home belonged on Stephen King's next one. Something like... *Dilapidation* by Stephen King. Undoubtedly, it would be a #1 bestseller, sold immediately to Hollywood, and star James Franco as a demonic real estate agent. The home, of course, would be a portal to hell, with each cupboard featuring imps and ghouls and gremlins. The devil himself—that is, if he were still alive—would come and go through the fireplace. Oh, and if his three-headed dog were still alive, too (it's not), it would undoubtedly be chained in the backyard.

"Enough about Stephen King already," said Allison, picking up on my thoughts and beeping her car locked as we headed for the "stairs." I glanced back at the Camry and its fresh scratch marks, winced inwardly, and decided not to mention how ridiculous it was that she had beeped the car locked, thus announcing to every ghost and goblin inside that we were here. "Although that book kinda sounds badass. Maybe you should write it."

I shook my head. "I'll leave the writing to my sister. She says she's working on a novel."

"But you write up your case notes."

"I do, and how did you know?"

"I can read your mind, silly."

I studied her closely, wondering if she had done more than just read my mind.

"No, Sam. I haven't read your case files. I've lived through most of them, remember?"

"Uh-huh. Watch your step."

"Trust me, I'll be watching every step from now on until I'm safely back in my car. And no, I'm not a drama queen."

"I hate that you can read my mind and I can't read yours."

"It's Millicent's rule."

"It's a dumb rule."

"No, it's not."

I sighed. She was right, of course. While I slept each morning, the bitch inside me had the ability to report back to others like her anything she might hear or see. Nothing was safe from her.

*Such. A. Bitch.*

Anyway, the late afternoon was bright and warm, and my beautiful sunlight ring was doing its job. Without it, I would have been slathered in sunscreen and sprinting up the suspect porch and into the suspect house. Without it, I wouldn't have been so casually strolling toward the "stairs." At present, a breeze swept over the clearing, swaying the branches of the surrounding trees and bending the nearby blades of grass. Remarkably, the lawn had been mowed within the week. Who mowed it, I didn't know, but I suspected I was about to find out.

"Maybe we should go up one at a time," suggested Allison. "You go first."

"Why me?"

"Because it's your house."

"Fine."

I took my first step up onto the "stairs" and was surprised when it didn't collapse under my New Balance shoes, although it groaned mightily. My next step was even more nerve-wracking, but by the time I'd climbed to the porch, I had mostly gotten used to the creaking and swaying. Behind me, Allison looked like a toddler taking her first tentative, unsteady steps. Never had I seen a human being's knees so wobbly before. By the time she reached my side, I was laughing hard enough to shake the whole porch, which made Allison reach for a railing that promptly broke off in her hand. I laughed harder.

"I wonder about you sometimes, Sam."

I wiped a tear. "It's funny."

"Not really."

"You're holding the railing in your hand. Your hand. The railing. I mean, it was good for absolutely nothing."

She shook her head and tossed said railing aside and, when I had gotten control of myself, we moved in single file over the warped floorboards and toward the front doors. Yes, I definitely heard scurrying beneath us, and the smell of skunk was pungent and ripe.

Amazingly, neither of our shoes broke through the wood. Then again, I had followed a path over an exposed 2x4, trusting that it would hold true, and it did. We avoided the obvious holes, and, once or twice, Allison squeaked behind me when something scurried in the holes beneath. I told her they were probably just cats. She said the "cats" had white stripes and stinky butts, and we both laughed. Dusty windows lined the porch, all curtained. The curtains, I noted, were mostly rags, and the windows were too dirty to see through. None were broken. I was tempted to cast my thoughts out and scan the area around us—which I can totally do, thanks to some weird inner radar system I'd discovered years ago. With a range of about twenty feet in any direction, it comes in handy.

But...

I resisted. I wasn't concerned or worried about anything within. My inner alarm wasn't pinging, and, truth be told, I wanted to be surprised by what I saw inside. This was, after all, my new home. Might as well experience it in all its dilapidated glory.

At the front double doors, each featuring plate glass and relief molding, I had just raised my right hand to knock—even while my left held the keys to the place—when the door creaked open slowly.

There, standing before us, was an elderly couple.

A smiling elderly couple.

# 4.

"You must be Samantha Moon," said the man.

"We've been waiting for you," said the woman.

"We're so pleased you are here," they said together. They stepped aside together, too, each to either side of the door, and each inviting us in with a grand sweep of their arms.

I looked at Allison. She looked at me.

*We don't have to go in there,* came her words in mind, just inside my inner ear, to be exact. *I mean we can run now and save ourselves.*

*They are a sweet old couple,* I thought back. *Besides, didn't you just face down a demon or three just a few months ago?*

*Honestly? These two are creepier.*

I laughed and stepped through the doorway... and into something entirely unexpected. The interior was, well, glorious, epic, and surreal.

And a little magical, too, if I had to guess.

Call me crazy, but the house seemed even bigger on the inside, as if the exterior, although large, had been an optical illusion. Scratch that. Not an illusion at all. I'd just spotted a number of candles hovering in mid-air. The candles were very much *not* attached to anything living—or dead for that matter. They were hovering as sure as I was standing here. Ah, now the candles were moving, drifting. As they shifted, shadows along the wall receded. And not just normal shadows. These were, I was certain, *living* shadows. Humanoid shadows. Yes, there were the hands. No, claws. And there were their eyes—red eyes, all. Heads that seemed to change shape as the shadows slithered over walls and fled the moving light.

A hand touched my shoulder and I jumped. Then the front door shut—not quite slammed, but certainly closed louder than necessary—and I jumped again. The hand belonged to Allison. The old couple stood at the door, smiling.

"You see the hovering candles?" Allison asked.

"Yes. You see the living shadows?"

"Yes. Does the home seem bigger than it should, Sam?"

"It does," I said. "Why are you holding me so tight?"

"Because I'm freaked the fuck out, Sam."

"Just ease up a little."

"Sam, is there anything holding the candles?" she asked, which was a logical question. "Like a ghost or something?"

"Nothing," I said.

"Shit."

Unlike me, Allison couldn't see into the spirit world. She could perform real magic, but seeing ghosts... not so much. Probably for the best. Seeing those buggers, well, everywhere, took some getting used to. Anyway, as we stood there, with Allison holding on to me, the elderly couple shuffled over the floor, which notably did not squeak or sway or sag, and stood before us. "Let me introduce us," said the man. "I'm Robert. And this is my wife, Mae."

"We are Robert and Mae," they said together.

I nodded. "As you know, I'm Samantha. And this is my friend, Allison."

I paused, waiting. Allison shuffled her feet.

*Say it with me,* I nudged her telepathically.

*No.*

*Say it.*

*Fine.*

*Ready?*

She mentally sighed. *Ready.*

"And we are Samantha and Allison," we said together.

Robert and Mae smiled brighter.

*Happy?* Allison asked me.

*Oh, yes,* I replied.

"Would you like a tour..." began Mae.

"...of your new home?" finished Robert.

"We would," I said.

"Thank you," added Allison.

The house was epic, to say the least. Easily bigger than Kingsley's and possibly even bigger than the massive Thurman estate on Skull Island in the Pacific Northwest. I counted no less than four hallways, each as long as the next. I also counted three stories, although there was a chance we might have come across a half floor which led to a painting studio full of, perhaps, the most macabre paintings I'd ever seen.

I spotted dozens of ghosts, and more of the red-eyed shadow people. A number of the floating candles followed us around, which was a bit unnerving. I asked about the candles, but neither Robert nor Mae would answer, and when I dipped into their minds, I saw something I'd never seen before: bright light and nothing more. No thoughts. No memories. No internal, running dialogue. Nothing but bright light.

The ghosts were typical fare, ranging from hazy outlines of their former selves to amorphous blobs with no shape or structure—just the crackling static energy that few would ever see. Yup, I'm one of the lucky ones. Allison wasn't so lucky.

*Thank God*, came her reply.

Truth be known, because my friend had continuous access to my own thoughts—well, when

I allowed it—she also had access to some of my memories. Usually the most recent of them. As such, she could readily see the ghosts as they registered in my memory banks, if she so chose.

*I don't so choose,* she thought. *I've seen enough weird shit in your thoughts to last me a lifetime. And when I say lifetime, I mean a normal, human lifetime. Sorry, was that mean?*

*A little.*

*Let's call it payback for all the teasing today.*

*Fair enough. And for the record, I've only been at this immortal business for over a decade. It doesn't feel much different than what it did before.*

*Have you ever been sick in the past decade?*

*Like with a cold?*

*Yes.*

*Nope.*

*Cramps? Bloating? Headaches? Toothaches? Sprained ankle? An ache here and there?*

*Nope and nope,* I thought.

*Bitch.*

I grinned as we continued the tour.

More rooms. More hallways. And another floor—the third floor. I was shown into the master suite that sported a four-poster bed and a massive semi-wraparound balcony complete with a lounge wicker chair, a glass table and metal chairs. The view from up here was extraordinary. Surely the best in all of Fullerton. Hills rolled this way and that, all dotted with homes. Many were surrounded with fences which, if you asked me, seemed completely un-necessary on a hill. Why fence off a freakin' hill? The view faced the south. Beyond the hills, in the hazy distance, were the mini-skyscrapers of Tustin and Irvine. Somewhere farther beyond was the beach, but I couldn't see it from here. Had I been in my dragon-bat form, I would have been able to see it. Talos's eyes were the shit.

The bed was well-used, the mattress saggy and ancient. If I knew Jeffcock at all, and I didn't, he didn't give a lick if the mattress was saggy or not. Like him, when I lay down my head at the butt-crack of dawn, I am out like a light, with the need for sleep overwhelming all of my other senses.

So, yeah, a bed was useless, really. Myself, I didn't need comfort to fall asleep. I just needed the arrival of the sun. And since I didn't wake up with a kink in my neck, I could just as easily sleep on a plank of wood. Or sleep standing up. Or sleep in a casket. Like a coming avalanche, daytime sleep was coming, whether I wanted it to or not.

There was a heavy-duty telescope on the balcony, complete with tripod, which I planned on taking full advantage of. There was an adjoining bathroom and a bathtub big enough for two. I almost—almost—imagined Kingsley and me in there, until I remembered where I was. This wasn't your everyday house. This wasn't even your everyday haunted house. This was a true house of horrors which, I suspected, hadn't yet given up its secrets. This was where a vampire reigned supreme, where he undoubtedly fed on many a victim, if the sheer amount of ghosts were any indication, and where an old couple had been cursed to continue to work and live, even long after their master's death, where enchantments held firm, and where other, darker, nastier entities dwelled. Most importantly, here dwelled the very vampire who had turned me, who had rocked my world, who had upended my world, a world that was still spinning out of control. Allison was right. This house was creepy. I should hate it, but I didn't. Was I comfortable? Not enough to imagine Kingsley and me in the tub, but certainly comfortable enough to imagine myself on the balcony, looking up at the stars with my new telescope.

"You are one freaky chick, Samantha Moon," said Allison, dispensing with the telepathy.

"I'm conflicted."

"You can't tell me you're seriously planning on living here? If so, I'm not sure how often I will be coming over."

"Then it's decided."

"Such a—"

"Don't say it."

"Bitch," she finished.

We continued the tour, moving through a number of rooms with their Jack-and-Jill bathrooms. All told, there were seven official bedrooms and a number of oddball, unclassifiable rooms, including lofts and spaces with wide double doors. Most bedrooms had their own balconies, although none of the views were as spectacular as the one off the master bedroom.

As the tour moved on to the kitchen, I asked the elderly couple some questions—who they were, how long they'd lived here, and what was the deal with the candles and red-eyed shadow people—and got officially zero response, that is, other than their smiling, happy faces. The good news, their smiling faces weren't indicative of possession. I knew this unofficially, of course, but their smiles were normal enough. Not stretched beyond their limits, as was often the case with demonic or satanic possession. Those hosting dark masters (i.e., me, Kingsley and a host of other vampires, werewolves and Lichtenstein monsters... and mermaids?) didn't sport the goofy grins. That was, I suspected, because we didn't host demons. Just dark masters.

No, these smiles were pleasant, normal, but completely devoid of any real warmth. That said, occasionally—just occasionally—I caught a flash of something more behind their eyes. Just a flash, and it was gone. It was, I was certain, their real selves, trapped within their own minds.

"What are your last names?" I asked again, hoping to find a sort of loophole in whatever mind-spell they'd been put under.

No response, although they might have smiled

brighter.

"Whatever mind control you are under is powerful, which surprises me, considering your former boss has been dead for six years."

"Our former master," corrected Robert.

"Er, right. How long did he live here?"

"Records will show that he purchased this home nineteen years ago," said Mae.

"Is that when you began working for him?"

No response.

"Do you have children?" I asked.

No response.

"Do you miss anyone?"

No response. Wait. No. Hmm. Maybe. Both of them glanced toward each other, or wanted to. But they stopped short.

"Do you enjoy living here?" I asked.

"We love it here, Ms. Moon," they said together.

"Do you really?" asked Allison next to me.

No response.

"Is there a way for me to end your enchantment?" I asked. "Is there a way I can help you go back to your normal lives?"

They said nothing, but both did slowly turn toward each other. As they did so, I felt my heart pick up a beat or two, which was the equivalent of it racing. I felt like a gamer who might have just unlocked a secret passageway into a secret room.

I looked at Allison; she looked at me. Slanting

sunlight came in through the window... and almost touched Allison's features, but not quite. It was as if the sunlight had hit a barrier of some type... and disappeared into it.

*There's a spell on the house, Sam. Inside it, too. I can feel it.*

*Can you help me break it?*

*I'm not good with spells, but Millicent is.*

*Because you're more the blast-first-and-ask-questions-later type of witch?*

*Something like that. I'll see what Millicent says.*

Millicent was, of course, one of three witches within Allison's powerful trifecta, of which I knew little since I was banned from their group—and also from Allison's mind. Not that I wasn't trustworthy... just that Elizabeth inside me most certainly wasn't trustworthy. Anything I knew, Elizabeth knew, and each night while I slept, Elizabeth was free to leave my body and return to what is known as The Void, the place where all the dark masters had been banished. There, she was free to commune with others of her kind, many of whom were presently possessing their own human bodies.

*Do you really think Millicent will help?*

*If I ask her to, yes.*

*Is she still a ghost?*

*She's in spirit, for now. But she's looking for a possible walk-in.*

*Walk in?*

*A host who is willing to leave their physical*

*body.*

*Who would do that?*

*Believe it or not, Sam, there are those who don't want to live on this planet, but are also not willing to take their own lives. The depressed, the down and out, the addicts, a number of them are willing candidates. They get to exit without dying.*

*And she just... takes over? But I thought she was pretty good at manifesting a temporary body.*

*She is, but it's limited. It's made of ectoplasm, not flesh and bones. It's limited and dissolves over time.*

*Okay, maybe I'm the one who should be afraid of her.*

"The master has left you instructions, Samantha Moon," said Robert.

"Within the instructions are the answers you seek," said Mae. "Or so he believed."

"And a way to break the spell?" I asked.

They said nothing. But Robert did peel away from the group and stepped out of the room. Meanwhile, Mae continued smiling at us. She was in her seventies, no doubt. Her skin was pale and smooth, with few wrinkles. It was almost as if they had been given a mild elixir to keep them youngish and healthy enough. But their age was undeniable.

*Can vampires be alchemists?* I asked Allison.

*I don't know, Sam. Seems unlikely.*

*What if they were alchemists before turning into vampires?*

*Seems a question for the Librarian,* she responded.

Meanwhile, Robert re-appeared in the kitchen, holding a rolled parchment of some type, wrapped with a leather cord. He stopped before me, bowed slightly, and handed it to me.

"Master wishes for you to read this at your earliest convenience, Ms. Moon."

I took it from him and frowned.

"Well, aren't you going to read it, Sam?" asked Allison.

I sensed her eagerness and curiosity. Myself, I wasn't so eager, although I was curious. Walking through the home of my attacker—my sire—was one thing. Seeing his things, his staff, his crazy enchantments was all within the realm of what I could handle.

Having him speak directly to me... well, that was quite another, and one I wasn't prepared to experience in front of anyone.

"Fair enough, Sam," said Allie, sighing.

Interestingly, something tugged at me from inside. Something that seemed to be... awakening, stirring within me. What that stirring was, I didn't know, but it was related to the letter. Or the scroll, or whatever the hell it was. Who writes on scrolls, anyway?

A five-hundred-year-old vampire does.

It was even sealed with wax, and stamped with an emblem, no doubt from a ring worn on his finger. The symbol in the wax was of a single flame. I expected this from Dracula. Then again, I didn't really know my sire, did I?

Nope. Not at all. Who he was, I didn't know. But the answers lay within this scroll. This overdone, melodramatic scroll. There was something else, something tugging at me. The answers were not entirely inside this scroll. They were within me, too, and how I knew that, I hadn't a clue.

"Are you okay, Sam?"

"I'm not sure."

"What's wrong?"

"I'm not sure of that either."

"Should we leave now?" asked Allison.

"I think so, yes."

And so we did, saying our goodbyes to the elderly, mind-controlled couple, even while the nearby candles floated up walls and into dark corners... keeping the seemingly always-present red-eyed shadow people at bay.

## 5.

I was at home, in my office, sitting behind my desk, with the rolled-up parchment resting in front of me—where it had been resting for the past thirty minutes now.

Instead of opening it, I found myself thinking about Allison.

I don't make friends easily. Scratch that. I don't make *close friends* easily, especially women. I'm not entirely sure why that is, but I've been aware of it my whole life. I get along better with men. I tend to have their sense of humor. I'm a tomboy at heart. I like to box and jog and dress in jeans and t-shirts and sneakers. In fact, up until I became what I am, I never wore much makeup. True, I loved my lip gloss, but the other stuff was... torture. Maybe it came from growing up with next to nothing, often living off the land, and often stealing food from our neighbors. My first job was at a cookie shop at age 14. I'd told them I was 16 and kept "forgetting" to bring my work permit until they quit asking. I brought home tons—and I mean tons—of broken and day-old cookies to my family. In fact, I think that was about when I started actually putting on a little weight... weight that stuck with me until I started the ultimate keto diet.

Anyway, throughout it all, I bonded with the local boys. I could play sports better than most, and I really, *really* liked to race the boys. I wasn't the fastest, but it was just so damn fun to feel the wind in your hair in an all-out dash to the finish line. Truth be known? I didn't think of myself as a girl. I was just me, and boys were my friends, and that was that.

Allison was my first true girlfriend. Crazy, I know. But she really is, and I wasn't entirely prepared for how needy she was. Or how touchy-feely she was. I was already standoffish at having anyone touch me, but she didn't give a damn if I was standoffish. Or cranky. She grabbed my hand with reckless abandon, or pulled me in for the mother of all hugs, all while I grumbled and cursed. Oh, and she made so many... noises. She *squeed* and clapped and giggled. My God, the giggling.

All of this was too much at times, and a part of me still rebelled at her girlishness. A part of me lashed out at her to keep her at bay, but Allison would not be denied. That, perhaps, was what I appreciated most about her. Her tenacity to be my friend, through thick and thin, through grouchiness and thinly-veiled snipes, was admirable. Truth be known, I didn't feel worthy of such devotion and friendship.

My reluctance to give out compliments and warmth was met with a hunger in her for both. Then again, maybe she was just naturally needy.

Which made me wonder...

Was Allison a kind of love slave, albeit of the friendly variety?

A few years ago, Russell Baker would have stolen for me, maimed for me, gone to prison for me, killed for me. His real self had slipped further and further away inside his own mind. But that connection had been sealed with sex.

Or so I had thought.

Was there some way that my proximity to Allison was causing an unwarranted devotion, a supernatural connection? Was Allison, in some way, my mental love slave? After all, hadn't she had clients today, and ditched them to come see me? She had. She had lost money she undoubtedly needed to come roam an old house with me. Then again, it was a home I'd just inherited from the very vampire who'd turned me. Surely that was of interest to her, right? Surely that was of more interest than training lazy middle-aged men who were trying to sneak peeks down her top.

Or so I told myself.

Hmm...

Hell, she had even brought me a Starbucks and a scone. Hell, she'd driven an hour to meet me... in terrible traffic, no less. Hell, I think I might be an ass.

Was I taking advantage of her friendship? But was her friendship more than friendship? Was I pushing things to see how far I could, in fact, push her? Or was I, actually, trying to push her away because I was afraid of getting too close to her? Hell, too close to anyone. Poor Kingsley was still chasing me. Granted, we have a very sweet relationship, but something else kept me from opening up to him completely and totally, although I did sometimes. Well, occasionally.

Of course, all fingers pointed directly at me and my inability to get close to anyone.

So was Allison simply being a "good friend" or was there something else here at work?

I didn't know, but I would keep an eye on things.

I drummed my fingers, cracked my neck. Glanced at the scroll. I checked my cell phone, cracked my knuckles, cracked my neck again. Stared at the scroll.

Yeah, it was time.

I didn't *have* to open it, of course. (Or, in this case, unroll it.) I could burn the scroll and never know what was ever written on it. I didn't have to enter the mind, so to speak, of the man who had turned me. Of the man who had attacked me, who had hurled me dozens of feet into a tree. I distinctly remember leaving my feet, of flying dozens—yes dozens—of feet through the air. And I very much remember hitting the tree which had knocked the wind out of me and broken some bones. I remembered the medallion on his neck, too, gleaming briefly. And I remembered his lips and teeth on my neck, the pain, the sounds of drinking... drinking! Gulping, even. And then, I remembered drifting away, so very certain I was going to die, of missing my kids already, of knowing, with certainty, that I was done with this world, and not knowing who had attacked me or why. Or, really, what was happening to me. Of course, I would awaken later in a hospital in Fullerton, bandaged and bruised... and healing far more quickly than anyone had a right to heal. Later, a man would be attacked in the hospital, a man I was certain I had fed from, but had no memory of that attack.

*Ugh.*

That had been nearly twelve years ago, and I could honestly say my life had never been the same since. Not even close. No, not at all.

*Is it ssso terrible, Sssamantha?* came a hissing voice deep inside my mind.

*Yes,* I thought. *And no.*

*Is it so terrible to be so strong, to be so powerful, to see the wonders of this planet? To see, in fact, the wonders of this universe?*

*Yes,* I thought. *And no.*

*Open the letter, Sssamantha. Open it...*

Elizabeth was always around. True, I could tamp her back into the further reaches of my mind, but she always found a way out. Always. Luckily, she kept in the background enough not to be a bother, and so these days I let her roam free. I let her participate, but from a safe distance. Truth be told, she sometimes... sometimes... gave me decent advice.

*The very fact that you want me to open it makes me think I should burn it.*

Hollow laughter drifted to me as if from down a distant hallway. *You are your own person, Sssamantha. I have long sssince known not to push or pressure you. Do as you pleassse. But know thisss. He was not one of us. No, not at all.*

Elizabeth obviously didn't know what was in the scroll letter, which I found curious. Something to keep in mind with vampires—and other such creatures—is that when you are dealing with them, you are, in fact, really dealing with *two* entities. The possessed (me, for instance)... and the possessor (Elizabeth, for instance). Sometimes, both entities worked in concert with each other, like Dracula and his own dark master, Cornelius. Others, not so much. I might fall in that latter category.

Dark masters, I knew, could roam at will while their charges slept. So each morning when I was floating through the cosmos, Elizabeth was back in the Void with her cohorts. There, the entities reported what they had seen, and, undoubtedly formed new plans... or carried on with the plans that were working. Surely, she would have known what my sire—that is, he who attacked me—had written in the letter? Surely, her own fellow dark master—that was, whoever was the entity who had possessed Jeffcock, would have reported in, so to speak.

*So to clarify,* I thought: *The man himself wasn't one of you? Or the dark master who possessed him wasn't one of you?*

*Over time, both.*

*You lost the dark master?*

*In a way, yes.*

*How? Why? What became of the dark master who possessed Jeffcock?*

*Two scenarios caused his defection. First, over time, he had become weakened by his regular consumption of cow and pig blood. Second, over time, he was convinced to give up the ways of our kind. And when Jeffcock was finally killed by the hunter, our one-time friend allowed himself to be caught.*

*Caught by whom?*

*The devil and his demons of course. He chose Hell, Sam.*

*But...*

*But only for a short while, of course. He knew, after all, a plan was in motion to do away with hell altogether. Now with hell abolished, he was in heaven.*

*There is heaven for dark masters?*

*Of course, Sam.*

At Jeffcock's death, the dark master who'd possessed him would have been ejected back to the Void. The Void, of course, is where all the dark master buttheads hang out while the rest of us—the possessed, that is—sleep our days away. Or, in my case, my mornings. Still, I was confused.

*What plan was underway to abolish hell?*

*You know the plan well, Sam.*

*Wait, what?*

*You effectively destroyed it.*

*No, I killed the devil.*

*Indeed, Sam. And now, his demons are on the run, too, scattered to the four corners of the earth. Tell me, who is guarding the gates of hell?*

*I, um, sort of thought it ran itself. And how do you know so much about hell?*

She laughed, and it was a grating, hissing, harsh, terrible sound.

*Few have escaped the reach of the devil, Sam. We are among them. We understood our enemy well.*

*The devil was your enemy?*

*Of course, Sam.*

*I would have thought Dark Masters and the Devil were a match made in heaven. Er, Hell.*

*Droll, Sam, even for you. Anyway, you would be*

*wrong. Although we appreciated the role he fulfilled and the fear he inspired, we had no use for him, and we bow to no one. We operated outside of space and time, and, as such, we knew what awaited for us at death. In particular, we knew the bastard would be there, waiting to escort us into a false hell. Really, he was a nuisance and nothing more. But a powerful one... and one that needed to be dealt with.*

*And now he's gone,* I thought, narrowing my eyes.

*And so he is.*

*Wait. Fuck. You can't honestly be saying...*

*No, Sssamantha. Even we are not powerful enough to orchestrate the downfall of the Prince of Darkness himself, especially with our limited access to physical bodies.*

I thought about that, and thought about it hard. When I'd first met the devil, he was searching for Danny. Hell, he'd even tricked me into finding Danny for him.

Elizabeth remained silent. I continued my thought process... Danny couldn't have escaped the devil if he hadn't been taught the ways of the dark masters—or at least, taught enough to avoid the devil and hell. Which he'd done, hiding inside my son, where he remains to this day. Except when Anthony transforms into the Fire Warrior and then, I assumed Danny hides out in the Void.

Elizabeth continued remaining silent. And when

the devil came sniffing around—well, when his three-headed dog came sniffing around—he saw something he'd liked. Or, rather, a *quality* he liked. But it had nothing to do with me. No.

*Good, Sam. Good. Yesss...*

It was my daughter's telepathy, her very powerful telepathy, that caught his eye. He'd said he could use her. Needed her, in fact.

*Fascinating...*

And when he lured my daughter away, I'd declared war on him.

*You did what you had to do to protect your daughter, Sam, and your family. Very admirable, Sssamantha.*

*Oh, shove it. The only reason he was interested in my daughter was because of the telepathic abilities she'd inherited from you. Well, not inherited, but you damn well know what I mean.*

*She was receptive to my gifts, you can say.*

*Fine. Whatever. You knew the devil was looking for someone like her.*

*Did I?*

*You did. But what I don't know is how you could have possibly known that I was in the* Book of All Living Things.

I felt a smile creep across inside of my skull.

*Your friend the Alchemist wasn't always the owner of the book, Sssamantha. Your friend the Alchemist—my dear son, by the way—was a meddling fool who took it upon himself to steal the most powerful of my books.*

*The books in the Occult Reading Room... are yours?*

*Of course, Sssamantha Moon. Some he collected over time, true. But most are mine. Mine...*

*That's why they call out to me...*

*No, Sssamantha. They call out to me...*

I blinked, shook my head, absorbing this information as best as I could.

*You... you helped orchestrate the downfall of the devil...*

*We helped facilitate it, Sssamantha. The downfall of the devil was all you.*

*And now your greatest obstacle has been removed.*

*You could say that.*

*But how does eliminating the devil help you?*

But before she could speak, I knew the answer.

*You don't have to run anymore*, I thought.

*No more running, Sssam. No, never again.*

*But you've been banished to the Void.*

*Temporarily, Sssam. Only temporarily...*

*And once you are free of the Void, you never have to fear the devil himself will drag you to hell.*

*You catch on quick, Sssam.*

*And you need me, of course.*

*You and only you can break down the walls of the Void. You, and only you...*

*Okay,* I thought. *Enough. Back in the box with you.*

*Sssee you soon, Sssister Moon.*

I shook my head and used the full power of my mind to collect her and bind her and drag her as far down as I could, where I locked her up in a heavy mental vault and threw up a few dozen virtual heavy-ass chains and a thick-as-hell imaginary padlock.

Rattled, I took a deep breath... and turned my attention to the rolled parchment.

The vampire who attacked me wasn't one of them, after all? And his own dark master spurned them for hell?

Okay, *now* I was interested.

Very, very interested.

## 6.

I slit the wax seal cleanly with my nail.

As I did so... something happened. Something stirred within me. Or was that my imagination? Still, my sluggish heartbeat picked up to not-so-sluggish. Hmm...

I unrolled the scroll and spread it out over my desk, holding it down with both hands.

Luckily, the paper wasn't made of weird and creepy materials, such as human skin. I'd seen human skin-bound books before. This wasn't it. But the paper was surely old, and the swooping penmanship was flawless... flowing and looping in some spots, tight and intense in others.

The author made bold and liberal use of space, with "f's" and "p's" and "j's" dipping low, well into the next line. His capital letters were grand and majestic and swooping, and his periods and punctuation marks were emphatic and deeply dimpled. The scroll was an orchestra and the author, its maestro. The flowing woodwinds and stringed instruments of lighter expository melded with the percussion of emphasis and emphatic explanation. It was all engraved with deeply grooved letters, furrows of sentences and lines that were easily seen from the opposite side of the parchment.

The man had a story to tell, and with my kids in the next rooms, gloriously going about their lives as if they were normal kids, I began reading the parchment before me...

It was, after all, not just written by someone who'd wantonly and brutally attacked me. No, it was written by someone far, far closer to me.

It was written by my father.

My one-time father.

# 7.

Dearest Samantha Moon,

If you are reading this letter, it means I am dead. Undoubtedly, I died tragically—and at the hand of the hunter known as Rand. I am aware that I have attracted his attention. He is human, yes, but I have heard of his prowess and success. Truthfully, I am a little more than concerned.

I am also familiar with his kind: that is, humans born to hunt, humans called upon to rid the earth of our kind, humans born of a hunting bloodline, of which I suspect my own nemesis is among. Be wary of such hunters, Samantha Moon. They have been the bane of our kind for centuries and will likely continue to be so. They add balance, I am told, which is necessary for life on earth to exist at all. With immortal killers comes also the fearless human hunters. Human but not quite human, either; after all, such hunters must be supernaturally sharp, skilled and driven. Their tracking is not understood, and their reflexes are second only to our own kind. Still, a well-prepared hunter can and will destroy the strongest of our kind. So, be wary, Sam.

Perhaps I should have heeded my own advice, eh? Sure, I have long since been dead by the time you read this letter; that is, had my own blood-sucking attorney done his job as advertised. You can never trust werewolves, Sam. Especially half-breeds. They make for damn fine attorneys, but they are a tight-knit bunch. They form smaller packs, but, ultimately, they are part of a much bigger pack, of which many willingly give their allegiance. Half-breeds straddle both lines, often with allegiance to both sides.

So we have established that I am quite dead, so dead that even my own attorney can safely deliver the news of my demise. Surely, you are surprised to have heard from me at all, let alone my attorney. I trust he has found you, no? Hopefully, you didn't wander too far off from your little home in Fullerton with its detached garage and big backyard and surrounding chain-linked fence. All new parents should have such fences. A wise choice, your little home, despite the fact that you had your misgivings about it. How do I know such things? Do I have to tell? Oh, I do? Well, as you might have guessed, I had been watching you for quite some time, well before your attack that fateful night. I knew you well, Samantha Moon. Better than you can possibly know.

Oh, Sam... where do I begin? There is so much to tell you, so much you should know.

Perhaps, then, I should begin at the beginning?

# 8.

And so he did.

Jeffcock Letholdus had been a farmer, a simple man with a simple family. They grew potatoes and harvested peat moss and fished the nearby rivers. It was a hard, clean, invigorating life. He and his family lived off the land, and, really, back in those days, there were few who didn't live off the land. Save for the nobility and warriors, who came through towns and took what they wanted, when they wanted, how much they wanted. The humble farmer accepted his fate, and those who fought back were made into examples.

Jeffcock did not accept his fate, and wished for freedom and peace. And so he moved his family far away and relied solely on their wits, ingenuity and themselves, and life was good. For a while.

After just one daughter, his wife grew barren. He accepted this; indeed, he was content with his only daughter, who he loved so very much, and she loved him in return, and they were a sweet little family who worked hard together, sung songs together, and told stories over fires together.

So many stories.

His daughter had a knack for the fantastical and was a clever girl. Her exposure to the outside world was nil, and so he often wondered where her stories of witches and werewolves, and of bloodsuckers and demons, had come from. She claimed they were from dreams and memories of another life, and he often laughed them off, although some chilled him to the bone.

In particular, his daughter seemed connected to the earth itself. Often, he found her not only playing with small animals, but surrounded by small animals. He would shoo them off, only to have her cry. Later, he learned to leave her alone with the animals that she often talked to as if, well, as if she were having *real* conversations with them. He and his wife just shook their heads and watched her commune with the creatures for hours upon hours. Later, his daughter would disappear into the forest and return with fistfuls of plants and herbs, claiming these would heal inflamed joints or fever, or still others were for stomach aches, runny noses, infection, and a number of others, for general good health.

He and his wife had heard of such plants, but never knew which was which, and, once, when he had been stricken with a pain in his side, his daughter had dashed off into the forest, only to return with a prickly plant that she claimed would heal his ailments. He had asked how she knew of this and she had said the animals had told her. As the pain increased, he had looked over at his concerned wife who had nodded once. And so, groaning and doubled over in bed, he allowed his daughter to make a tea of the pungent plant. After his first tentative taste, he'd found the concoction bitter. It had gone down smoothly, though, and his body seemed to accept it willingly. And so, knowing he was in bad shape, and trusting his little girl with his very life, he had gulped down the hot tea, and prepared himself for a long night of pain... perhaps many long nights.

The relief wasn't quite instant, but sometime in the night it came. Sweet, blessed relief. His daughter had him drink one more follow-up cup of brew a few hours later, and by morning he was back in the field working, astonished by the unlikely help he had received from his daughter... and the animals, herself no more than five years of age.

Later, he had paused in his morning routine, leaning on his rake, and watched his little girl skip off into the forest, followed by squirrels who dashed down trunks, birds who flew behind her, and a bobcat who came slinking around a boulder. The bobcat had made him nervous, granted, but his daughter had assured him over and over again that the big cat was the wisest of all.

Years later, tragedy had struck.

His wife, who often ignored the pleadings of their daughter to drink this tea or chew on that root, grabbed her heart shortly after finishing dinner one evening. Seconds earlier, he had just looked out the window, and spotted their child rushing out of the woods and across their fields, when his wife gasped from over the sink, clutched at her chest, looked at him pleadingly, then sank to the floor in a heap. He had just rushed to her side when his daughter burst through the structure's only door. Together, they fought to keep her alive, doing all they knew to do. His daughter, crying and shaking, rushed around the home to prepare a special tea, but his wife was already long dead. As his little one tried to tip a not-so-hot brew into her mother's partially open mouth, he held the woman he loved in his arms. The tea spilled out, and, after further attempts, he gently took the mug from his daughter's hand and pulled her into him, too, and together they held the woman they called mother and wife. They held her throughout the evening and into the night. Finally, he picked up his child, who had cried herself to sleep, and carried her over to her bed against the far wall.

While his daughter slept, he buried his mate of nearly two decades in the back of the field, near a ring of stones. It was where she had asked to be buried a year or so earlier. She was young and he had only shrugged and agreed, dismissing the request. Well, he didn't dismiss it now, and it had been hard shoveling the wet sod upon the face of the woman he had come to love, even if it had taken a few years for him to find the love.

Come morning, his child had wailed even louder to discover her mother gone and buried, but he had felt it important to not subject the little one to the nastiness of the grave. He had held her and soothed her, even as she had beat upon his chest and pulled at her own dark hair. This had gone on all day and well into the night, until finally, she had cried herself to sleep again. After that, she spoke little of her mother, and he followed suit.

For many years after, they lived a solemn, somber existence, although his daughter still wandered off into the forest, still claimed to speak to animals, but now, she also added "forest spirits," of which he had heard rumors of all his life but never believed, until now. After all, his daughter was gaining an education, from whom, he did not know. Imagine his surprise, then, when one day, she returned with a book she claimed to have found wrapped and bound in a nook of a tree, a book given to her by one of the forest spirits, a book that she, amazingly could read.

He himself could not read. Nor had his wife.

And yet...

He watched in amazement as his daughter pored over the unusual book with chicken-scratch writing and colorful pictures, all wrapped in vellum of the finest quality. He watched her close her eyes and commit what she had learned to memory. Often, he caught her reciting what she had read. And oftener still, he found her at the kitchen, brewing twigs and leaves and roots. Some things she wrinkled her nose at, others she smiled at approvingly. Once or twice he asked what she was doing, but both times she smiled and said she was only keeping herself busy.

Never did she forgive him for burying her mother without at least giving her a chance to say goodbye. He regretted his act of mercy and realized his mistake. Every day after, he nearly dug up his beloved to give his daughter the goodbye she needed, but as the days piled on, the chances of that happening grew less likely, until he was certain the corpse was little more than a dried husk. Digging her up would do more harm than good, surely.

And so it was with a heavy heart that he watched his daughter grow more and more distant, although he was pleased to see she had found a hobby that so interested her. She still performed her duties around the farm and in the peat bogs, helping him remove the heavy bricks, to be used for fuel in wintertime. His daughter insisted that he only take fallen branches and trees from the forest, and even then, she was careful to point out which he could use. Some, he would learn, were home to her many friends and were off-limits. He smiled and sighed, allowing her to have her way. It was, after all, more important to her than him. Besides, the mossy peat bricks often provided more than enough fuel.

She was beginning her teen years when she told him she was a witch, and she had been such a witch for many lifetimes before, or so she was told by the forest spirits. This lifetime was just one of many, and the animals and spirit friends helped her remember. She was good at being a witch and loved the connection to all things it provided. She loved the power of it, too, and wanted to do good work in the world.

"What kind of work, little one?" he had asked.

"I want to help the weak and poor."

"'Tis an honorable ambition."

She had nodded and said two more would come. He had asked what that meant and she had shrugged and said the spirits had told her that individually they were strong, but together, they were powerful. Together they could move mountains, literally.

She had asked if he feared witches and he said he did not understand them, but did not fear them, and if his precious little girl wanted to become one (*was one*, she had corrected) then being a witch, he believed, was the greatest thing he could imagine. She had hugged him then, and he sensed she had been afraid he would not accept her. He had hugged her back and when she laid her head on his shoulder for the first time in many years, he told her he was so sorry for not allowing her to say goodbye to her mother, that it was his greatest regret, and if she could ever forgive him, he could die a happy man.

She held him tighter and he felt her own hot tears on his neck, and as the wind slapped at their front door and found the small fissures in the planks, wafting over the fluttering candles, she asked if he could ever forgive her in return.

As the wind howled and the rain drummed against the panes and roof, they held each other like that for a long, long time...

# 9.

I continued reading, his flowing penmanship confident and sure, his words leaping from the page and into my heart:

I watched my daughter come into her own.

She was growing into a fine young lady, beautiful and full of life. I would like to say much like her mother, but my little one was oh-so-different. Shorter, for one, with raven-black hair compared to her mother's shiny auburn. My little one was connected, alert and alive. My wife, ah, well, she was content to stay indoors and take care of us, which she did very well, bless her heart. More often than not, my daughter would return home with twigs in her hair, dirt on her cheeks and elbows and knees, skipping and humming a song of her own creation. Or a song she'd heard the spirits sing. I could listen to her sing all day, and often I did, pausing my work to tilt my head and listen to her lilting voice carry over fields and meadows, through woods and dale.

My life was peaceful, perfect. My little princess was straddling worlds and I was okay with that. She was unlike any young girl I'd ever seen. I neither dared to change her nor wanted to. I knew she was different, and I knew she was a witch. A real witch. A trained witch, in fact. Trained by whom, I never could ask. And she was only growing stronger.

Her trifecta of witchy friends never did arrive; at least, not in time.

Instead, someone else—or something else—came for her.

You have to know that in those days, the Inquisition was going strong, but I had believed we were far removed from it. Indeed, we had no neighbors to speak of, living simply and humbly in the deep forests. We grew our own food and ate from the land. I gave up my hunting at the urging of my daughter, which was fine by me. Anything for her. Always, anything for her. She was my guiding light in this world, tapped into a knowing that I was not privy to, but all too willing to learn from. She was my beacon, my angel, and she was wise beyond her years. If she told me that eating meat blocked our connection to the land, then I believed her. Besides, I was pretty sure she was friends with every single animal in the fields and stream, anyway.

Little did I know that the Inquisition didn't just have eyes and ears everywhere, but they employed the supernatural, which was ironic indeed.

Little did the Church know that their greatest tracker was consumed by dark forces. Perhaps the darkest of forces, for he is pure evil, Samantha Moon, and something that, having seen firsthand, few, if any, can stop. Worse—if there can be anything worse—he is supernaturally drawn to the most powerful of witches. Meaning, there is no escaping him. Indeed, I would go on to discover that this one entity was responsible for the demise of the world's greatest witches and warlocks.

Including you, Samantha Moon.

\*\*\*

I immediately dropped my awl and hammer when I'd heard the scream.

When I heard *you* scream.

Yes, you, Samantha Moon. For my little one was none other than you, born into one of your many reincarnated forms. I was lucky enough to be your father in one of them.

That said, I'd never heard such a scream before, full of bloody murder and terror and furious, spitting anger.

Fast, I ran, tripping once and falling straight to

my face. I scrambled to my feet, feeling as if my life was about to be forever changed for the worse, you screamed again, and again, and all the forest seemed to scream with you. Birds erupted and animals scrambled from far and wide. I was only mildly surprised to see your friend the bobcat dash past me, and head in your direction. The wind picked up, too, howling mad as I ran faster and faster, and I just caught sight of you at the back of a horse, a massive arm reaching back and holding you in place, the red-hooded rider bigger than anyone I'd ever seen before, and his black steed clearly not of this world. You thundered off into the woods, reaching your arms back to me, even as you beat against the unmovable arm of your captor.

He rounded a bend as your screams trailed behind. And then, the screams stopped abruptly.

I ran, sobbing and hysterical, until I rounded the same bend... and came across something most unusual indeed. The deep hoofprints of the devil steed had stopped suddenly... and seemed to vanish into thin air. The creature had been there one minute, and gone the next. I searched every direction, certain the horse had made a great leap to throw me off the trail, but there were no prints to be found, anywhere.

And just like that, you were gone.

My angel girl was gone, and I was left alone searching for prints that did not exist, surrounded by the braying and sorrowful sounds of the many animals left behind, but none were more lost and tortured than my own hoarse voice calling out to you.

Calling, calling...

## 10.

He would immediately abandon the home in the woods and all my belongings and set out in search for me—or the young girl he claimed was me.

(I still wasn't convinced.)

He never returned home. Indeed, he would spend many days and nights traveling and questioning any and all he came across—"had they seen the red-robed man or his raven-haired daughter?" He rarely stopped for rest and only did so when his body demanded it. He only ate when the hunger finally overwhelmed his desperation and rage. And only then, he would eat a few berries or some stolen mutton. After all, he had no money. After a week of searching and questioning, roaming from hillside to hillside, town to town, he had finally come across a man who knew of the red-hooded hunter.

The man was a priest, and a very old one at that, who spoke his mind with nary a care of what others thought of him, let alone the Church itself.

The priest had overheard the desperate father asking any and all who would listen to him, beseeching passersby in the street, if anyone, anywhere, had seen the red-hooded man. None had, or none admitted to having seen him. Just as he'd been about to move on to the next street corner, a strong hand grabbed him about the shoulder and pulled him into a side alley. Weakened with hunger and beside himself with grief, he went stumbling along easily enough.

The old clergyman had veritably held up the stricken father; indeed, he had shaken him, too, perhaps harder than necessary. Once he'd gotten Jeffcock's attention, the old man had proceeded to tell a tale that had chilled the searching father to the bone, a tale that dropped him to his knees where he could be found for many hours afterward.

The man whom Jeffcock sought was not someone the priest approved of; indeed, the old priest downright protested the man's involvement, questioning his virtue, and suspecting the motivation was far more sinister than the Church was willing to admit. The old priest was but a simple vicar in a backward town on the far edge of nowhere. Who would listen to him? But he'd seen the man in question in action, and the priest had felt the wickedness, the vileness, the evil radiating off him. It had been only a brief glimpse, but it had been enough to convince the priest that the man was not really a man, but something else, something sent by the devil himself.

\*\*\*

In Jeffcock's words:

I would go on to hear many such stories of this man who was not a man, this ultimate hunter of witches and warlocks, and, with each story, my blood would boil, and I would continue my own hunt with ever-increasing desperation.

Another priest who was in the know had told me that this red-hooded man operated outside of the Inquisition, that he'd been retained to bring to justice the real witches of the New and Old Worlds. Indeed, I would learn that, in general, that the Inquisitors, as a whole, highly doubted the veracity of real witchcraft—they saw it as merely a superstition and nothing to take too seriously. This, of course, goes against general wisdom. Believe it or not, witches were not a target of the Inquisition, although there had been some famous trials. "Witchcraft as a nuisance" was the general rule of law.

Surprisingly, the Inquisition was rigidly overseen, with witnesses, tribunals, confessions and torture. And, yes, executions, although those were few and far between. Even the torturers, believe it or not, were held to some standard of decency... and were even given time limits. The Inquisition was far tamer than was led to believe, and not all witches were burned at the stake. Many were simply tortured and sent home.

None of that mattered to the red-hooded rider, who began his career as a torturer, and later, an executioner. There had been many instances when the man had gone rogue, going against the decisions of the tribunals and overseeing mass executions. He'd been punished and imprisoned, but managed to escape, and he'd been on the run ever since.

It is here where his story gets murky. By most accounts, the man seemed... possessed, deranged, and, in the least, obsessed beyond all reason with witches. He'd claimed witches were real—not just a nuisance, which was the Church's official stance—with real power, who should be hunted and killed without the benefit of trial, without the opportunity of renouncing Satan.

Despite having a price on his own head, he continued his work... somehow managing to find, torture and execute witches, leaving a trail of misery from village to village. By all accounts, he tortured and executed in private. His victims were often found scattered far and wide, most burned at makeshift stakes, others gutted and left to bleed to death. He was truly the judge, jury and executioner, and the death of witches everywhere. Real witches, that is. Those with real power, a real connection to Mother Earth. You were one of them, my child.

So, then, how does this man work? From where did he come from? And where did he go? How had he managed to avoid the price on his own head, find the witches he feared, and then, disappear again? Good questions, and I have spent my life searching for the answers—and searching for him.

To make a long and terrible story short, I did eventually find you. I'd followed clue after clue, whispered rumor after whispered rumor, until I happened upon what could only have been called the hooded rider's stronghold: a cave on the outskirts of a remote town, a place where some locals had heard the galloping of horses' hooves in the dead of night, a cave known to have been haunted and terrible, from which screams and foul smells emanated. Only the bravest had ventured in, and none had returned.

Now, months after your abduction, I ventured fearlessly into the cave, armed with sword and knife and crossbow. At this point, one could have called me deranged, so sure was I that I was tracking the devil himself.

He wasn't there, nor his horse, although I had seen evidence of both. No, I didn't find him, but what I did find was a nightmare of the worst kind.

Deep within the cave was a pit, and within the pit was a gruesome pile of the dead. Many were burned and charred, others had been gutted and mutilated. The stench was overwhelming and it was unlike anything I'd come across—that is, until I came across another of the hooded rider's execution chambers. And another. And another.

Horrified and sickened, fighting tears and vomit, I searched the gruesome pit... only to see you there, sweet girl, high atop the pile of the dead, yourself having suffered terrible wounds of which I will not describe here. Needless to say, only part of you was there.

I fished you out and gave you a decent burial in the woods nearby. I picked a spot where I could also see the cave entrance, and there I sat with you, day and night for many weeks, eating off the land, drinking from a nearby stream, and altogether going hungry, waiting for the red-hooded man to return. But I didn't see him again, not then. Neither him nor his devil horse.

And so it was with great sorrow that I eventually left you there in the woods, by the cave entrance. But I left a changed man. I was no longer the meek and humble farmer I had been prior to your abduction. I was a man filled with rage and a thirst for revenge, a man destroyed by grief, a man with little care in the world other than finding your killer. What he'd done to you... ah, it still brings tears to my eyes, little one.

Yes, the red-hooded man would pay, whoever he was. He would pay with his life, even if it was the last thing I ever did.

Little did I know who I was up against, and who this foul creature was. Or, rather, who he would evolve into. Yes, he'd been human... once. But no more.

What he became, well... I was about to find out.

## 11.

I will not bore you with the details or the madness of obsession that consumed me in the following years.

But my search for the man who I came to know as the Red Rider, took me far and wide across a plague-infested Europe. How I didn't succumb to the disease was a miracle in and of itself. I suspect my will alone kept me alive, my hunger for revenge. No way in hell I was going to allow the black death to stop me from finding my daughter's murderer. And so I searched, following his clues and his trail of destruction.

My problem: the man was a ghost, as I had witnessed upon his abduction of you. He could seemingly appear and disappear at will, and how does one find such a man? I didn't know, but I was going to figure it out. I had to. I had to find him. I had to avenge your death. Never did you deserve such an assault. Never.

My God, Sam... what he did to you...

As I traveled, I cursed God. I also cursed myself for not keeping a closer eye on you, or finding you in time. Surely, I was only days away from locating you, perhaps even hours, judging by the condition of your partial remains. Ugh, I can't think about that now. But thinking about it then drove me through filthy streets and back alleys, through snow and rain, through hunger and lack of sleep, through plague and war.

Through, quite frankly, madness.

Never had I known such grief and anger, and never had I wanted to kill someone so much. Killing him, I knew, would not bring you back, but revenge was all I had, and it was my lifeline.

I would soon learn, this was no man I was hunting.

Sure, he had started out as a man. But he had become something else, something beyond imagination. Who else could disappear in such a manner? Who else could have possibly found you, in such remote backcountry? My God, we lived alone in the woods, far removed from anyone.

Again, I will spare you the tediousness of my investigations, but know that I would discover, over time and many inquiries, that he was a warlock himself, and a very powerful one. Perhaps the most powerful. Once, he had been the chief consultant to the Grand Inquisitor of Spain, a man who had seen the works of real witches and feared them, a man who dabbled in the dark arts, too. He was a true example of a man who feared and hated what he most wanted to become. I would learn more about him over time, but most of what I know, is only supposition.

I suspect he had been a natural warlock, much like you had been a natural witch. I suspect his parents and those around him were not as amenable as I had been. I suspect the magic had been beaten out of him to the point he hated, feared and was envious of all who could perform it. Perhaps he hated himself. Perhaps he was making amends for any "evil" he had performed. Perhaps he loathed himself unlike any man had ever loathed himself. Mostly, I think, he feared what he could become, what was waiting for him just beneath the superficial surface.

But something happened to him as he caught and burned the real witches of the world. He would become more and more powerful. With each death, his strength increased. Later, and this is based on the physical evidence found in his wake, he would discover that consuming the witches would give him greater strength still.

Yes, Sam. Feasting upon their flesh like a true ghoul.

As the years progressed, he would discover he

did not age, and this was because of the magic flowing through him; no, not his own magic, for witches are not immortal. No, it was the accumulated magic of those he killed and consumed. The magic kept him young. It also kept him alive, and so he renewed his killing spree in earnest, killing the best and the brightest of the witches and warlocks, while he himself grew more and more powerful, all while he rid the world of its true protectors: the witches who could watch over the land.

As the years piled on, the bones of his victims were picked clean... and even the bones themselves were consumed. I had seen evidence of all of this and more. Like vampires and blood, he cannot exist without such consumption. And so this thing, this devil, seeks the truly magical among us, consuming all they have become. It is why, dear girl, you would spend the next several lifetimes to reclaim the magic you once held, for once it's gone, it needs to be built back up. You were game, and in each subsequent lifetime after your murder, you gained more and more magic. How many lifetimes since your attack? Four, by my estimate, although I was not always successful in locating you. In each, as far as I could tell, you didn't pursue your witchy calling. After all, the magic was weak... but growing stronger. I do believe in this lifetime you were close to reclaiming your birthright; indeed, the trifecta of witches of whom you had often been a part, were gathering again. But, alas, the trifecta was not meant to be. Your attack six years ago effectively erased the magic within you, snuffed it out as surely as a blast of cold air upon a lighted candle.

As you might know, vampires and magic do not mix. At least, not with the kind of earth-based magic you'd once mastered over many lifetimes, not the kind, loving, benevolent magic you used to heal the earth, to heal the animals, to heal others, and to play with endlessly. Sadly, there is nothing loving about the dark masters who inhabit us, Sam Moon. Sure, there are the rare cases where a dark master and its host have a pleasant-enough relationship. I know of such a case in the state of Washington, although she is not like us, Sam. No, she prefers the sea, a shifter. Last I heard, she is a private investigator, too. Perhaps you should look her up?

How do I know so much, you ask? I have lived nearly 500 years, Sam. I have lived and I have sought answers continuously. I have hidden in shadows and watched. I commanded answers from unwilling humans, and I have read the darkest of books. I have sought the most spiritual among you, too, and I have asked the big questions. But always I searched for two things, and two things only:

I searched for you in your many incarnations.

And I searched for the Red Rider.

But I digress...

The dark masters, as you may or may not know,

were practitioners of the dark arts, Sam. I say 'were' because they are gone now, Sam. Banished to another realm, The Void, I believe it is called. Again, I digress...

The dark masters were experts in the blackest of magic. In many ways, they paralleled the devil and his demons. In many ways, they were more powerful than the devil and his demons. In others ways, not so much. The devil had dominion over death; they did not. And so they fled the devil, and they do so until this day. I have heard rumors that a great plan is in place to destroy the devil and his demons. But I am not willing to believe it possible, although I have been wrong before. Truth be known, the devil is one of the few entities who keep the dark masters in check. He, and the alchemists, those brave warriors of the light.

Yes, the magic was taken from you, Sam. But you are so much more than magic. You have always been inquisitive. You have always been a helper, a healer, a voice for the weak. After your murder and subsequent loss of magic, you often worked in the fields of medicine. And, although the magic had been taken from you, no one could take from you your inherent knowledge of the earth and its natural remedies. You healed the sick, and they often came to you from miles—and countries—away. In this life, you chose another path. You chose to fight crime, and that is admirable indeed. Now, I see you work independently as a private investigator, and I could not be more proud of you. Surely, you could have gone down the darkest of paths, but you are fighting it, fighting the natural inclinations of the evil that resides within you.

And, Sam, make no mistake. She is the evilest, and most vile of them all. Be careful there.

How did I become who I am—a vampire—and how did I come to find you in yet another incarnation?

To answer each, I must take you back to the life in which you were taken from me and destroyed by the Red Rider, the life in which I had been blessed to be your father.

But first, let me clarify... for I sense your confusion even now as I write these words, years before you will read them, if at all. I say 'if at all,' because, well, who knows? Perhaps I will survive the hunter's attack. Perhaps I will keep on living as I have lived. If so, then I will find another way to reach you. After all, I never planned on leaving you this note. No, I had planned on sitting with you and holding your hands and gazing into your eyes—my daughter's eyes—and telling you all of this in person, if you would have me.

Why haven't I, then? Your wounds are too fresh, I suspect. You are too new to this way of life. You are, quite, frankly, too green and inexperienced to understand all that I am going to lay upon you now. You need to experience what you are. You need to be open to the truth. I was—and am—

willing to wait. After all, we now have eternity to reconnect.

Yes, I am chuckling over here. I say an eternity, but really, I am just a silver arrow away from losing everything, including you.

And so here I am, writing this letter, hoping beyond hope that you will be ready to read it when the time comes. If that time comes, I will be long gone, and so this letter is all I have. Now, I need to clear the air, for I sense your confusion and, possibly, your anger... even if only in my imagination.

No, Sam. It was not I who attacked you that night six years ago. It was another, one whom I destroyed, one who had the vilest of intentions for you. The attack was already under way when I arrived... and you were dying in my arms, your throat torn open. I had only one option to save you...

But, alas, I am getting ahead of myself.

Let me backtrack.

Let's go back to that cave, when I found your partially-consumed body. Yes, Sam. The monster feasted on you as an animal would. But he had taken more than the flesh from your bones. He had stolen from you your heritage, your birthright, your soul-right. He had stolen from you your magic, and discarded you with the others.

And he had moved on to his next victims.

I had been forced to move on, too.

Gone was my need to find you.

Only to be replaced with a need to avenge your

death.

No, I did not yet know what monster I faced yet, but over the years, decades and centuries, I would learn more about this foul beast. And the more I knew, the more I wanted to hunt him. Needed to hunt. The more I knew, the more I knew he had to die.

But with time, comes age... yes, Sam, I would spend the rest of my natural life looking for this devil. And I was dying.

And I couldn't have that.

No, not at all.

## 12.

The life I had known is long gone. So far away now that sometimes I wonder if it was ever real. But you are real, and so I know it had to be true.

Imagine thinking back to your earliest days in school, Sam. Only a few decades ago, if I am correct. Now, imagine going back ten decades. Twenty. Thirty. Fifty. Sometimes I think humans are given only seven or eight decades or so because the memories are too numerous. But they are all in here, Sam. Sometimes I confuse them. Sometimes I need prompting, and sometimes I don't remember at all. I am certain I have forgotten whole decades, let alone years.

But I remember what I need to remember, and I remember you, and I remember my first wife. Yes, I say first. There would be more, some mortal, and some immortal. There would be many close acquaintances, and many friends, too, although these days, I am friendless, which is fine by me. These days, I am not of a mood to connect, to entertain, to pretend. These days, I know my time is short, and I have business to do. This letter is such business.

Besides, do I not have Robert and Mae? Perhaps you have met them by now? I suspect so, since they were instructed to give you this note... or scroll. What can I say, I'm old-fashioned. Yes, Robert and Mae... who are they? I haven't a clue, Sam. They came with the house. They are immortal, I think. They might also be ghosts. Living ghosts, if that's possible. They don't say much and their minds are nothing but light, but they are all the company I need. The red-eyed shadow men, not so much. They, too, came with the house. I could do without them, which is where the enchanted candles come in.

I was in my late thirties when I lost you, Sam. Forty futile years of searching later, I found myself in my late seventies—and no closer to finding your killer. My time, quite frankly, was running out.

By this point, I was weak of body and mind. Years of hunting your killer had stolen my health. My body was broken and sickly and I had "the cough," which is what we called it back in the day. Tuberculosis is what it is called today. My time was running short, and I knew I would die, not only never having avenged your murder, but never having really seen the Red Rider again. Sure, I had gotten close. I had seen evidence of his presence—the missing girls, mostly. And five or six other times I had come across his kill caves, as I've come to call them.

Knowing your killer was still out there, feeding on the innocent and destroying families, was a tough pill to swallow. I nearly said, stone to pass, but that was a saying from another time, another place, although undoubtedly still relevant today.

But my spirit was strong, even if my body was weak and dying, and so when I found myself in a familiar city—indeed, my search for the Red Rider often took me in meandering circles, an idea occurred to me.

You see, Sam, by this time, I had spoken to many mystics and witches and warlocks, and those of indefinable lineage. I had spoken to dozens, if not hundreds, of those who fled—and would later die—at the hands of the Red Rider. And I had spoken to those who would later burn at the stake. Sam, I had seen and interacted with the undead. I was sure of it, although few would give me straight answers. Indeed, upon my travels, I had heard the whisperings of werewolves, merfolk and vampires. Of elves and imps and fairies. But it was that first grouping who held my attention; in particular, the vampire.

I was very, very interested in living forever. In

the least, a few dozen more years... however long it took for me to track down the Red Rider. Indeed, I would have welcomed death the next week, if it meant that I had banished the earth of this fucking monster. Pardon, my language.

And so, weakened and dying, and wondering if I would ever get close to the creature who had proven shockingly elusive (one who could vanish into thin air), I sought out a man I had seen years earlier feeding upon the broken body of an alley cat. And not just feeding, but drinking deeply from a gaping wound in the animal's neck.

Drinking, Sam. Nay, *gulping*.

Never will I forget the image. Nor had I forgotten the way he had wiped his lips and licked the ichor from his fingers. Interestingly, he'd exited the alley with the dead cat, all while I'd been sleeping nearby in a darkened nook of the alley; well, that is, until the sounds of slurping and drinking had awoken me.

Fascinated and repulsed, I had wondered if this man—if he was a man—was one of the undead I'd often heard whispered of. I both believed it, but didn't believe it, either. If I hadn't seen evidence of another man having disappeared before my own eyes—with you, no less—I would have been less inclined to believe such tales. Then again, had I been hunting a mortal man, I would have surely found him by now... and killed him.

From near the opening into the alley, I had

watched the man cross a cobbled street, and then cut through a nearby park. Weak and dying, I had done my best to follow him. At one point, I spotted him bending down. I paused, not daring to get any closer. When he'd finally moved off, I waited some more, then inched out from the tree I'd been using for cover. A hundred stumbling paces later, I spotted a small, fresh mound, where, I was certain, he'd buried the cat.

I blinked, confused. Never had I suspected ghouls to be... sympathetic?

Was it possible?

I didn't know, but footprints led further into the woods and, against my better judgment, I followed the prints. They led out of the park, into the surrounding woods, and continued on for some time until I spotted a stone building high above, alive with candlelight in its many windows. It sat alone upon a hill, and, with the very last of my strength, I followed a well-worn path all the way to the vampire's lair above...

## 13.

Whoever lived there had, undoubtedly, heard me from many hundreds of yards away, if not a half mile or more, with all of my coughing and clamoring.

At one point I stumbled and fell and lay there in the mud and rain, wondering if I could ever find the will to move again, wondering if I should just give it up and let go. After all, the Red Rider had proven frustratingly elusive. Who was I to think I could find him? Besides, wasn't I at the end anyway? And what choice did I have in the matter? None, of course. Death was staring me in the face. Hell, if I didn't turn away from this muddy puddle, I would drown right here. A lifetime spent on revenge... only to be extinguished by a two-inch puddle.

The water before me sizzled and bubbled with

the driving rain. Despite my warnings, I inhaled some of it and coughed—only to inhale more of it. For the life of me, I couldn't turn away from this damned stupid death.

I tried pushing myself up, but couldn't.

I sucked in more water. Coughed again; inhaled still more.

My feet kicked and I knew I was suffocating.

*Terrible*, my mind raged. I search all these years only to die... like this. Whether I drowned now, or somehow turned away from the puddle, I was going to die on this night. Of that, I had no doubt.

It was then, Sam, that I heard the words. Words that I was certain I had hallucinated. After all, I had not breathed in over a minute, nor could I find the strength to push myself up... let alone roll over away from this damnable puddle. My body, quite frankly, was sick, old, worn down, and diseased. Death was welcome. But not like this. No, never like this.

This was my frame of mind when the words came, and they came incessantly:

*Come to me, and I will help you.*

The words had seemed foreign to me. Then again, dying was foreign to me, too. Perhaps my mind was spinning out of control, losing it completely. Perhaps even Jesus himself was calling to me to heaven, although I doubted it. One could not be as filled with hate and rage as I, and be received with open arms by the Son of God.

The devil, I had thought next.

It was the devil calling to me.

Yes, that made more sense. I had neglected my body my mind, my life, my health, my sanity, in search of your killer. I had neglected my faith, too. I had renounced it all for one single act of revenge that had been denied to me.

*Come to me, and I will help you.*

The words came again, and again.

I coughed more, and now my lungs were full of the stuff, so full that I couldn't find the air to cough again.

By sheer coincidence—perhaps the wind shifted, perhaps the blasted puddle water shifted, too, or perhaps I found it within—I found my head above the water. In that instant, lightning flashed, illuminating the night sky, and, remarkably, I caught a glimpse of the stone manor silhouetted against trees and stars. My eyes also found a small, dimly-lit window, where stood a dark figure watching me.

No, not standing. He was leaning out, bracing his hands on a ledge, watching me intently.

And not just watching, I would realize later. But reaching out to me with his own mind.

My lungs seized as I searched for breath, too weak was I to even cough up the water. My too-heavy head splashed down again, and bubbles appeared before me. And a light, too. A bright light.

*Who are you?* I asked the light.

*The one you seek.*
*The man in the window?*
*You think me a man?*
*Are you not?*
*Come to me, and you will know.*
*I'm dying.*
*I know.*
*He killed my daughter.*
*I know that, too.*
*And you will help me?*
*Yes.*
*How?*
*What is it you seek?*
*The Red Rider.*
*What else?*

My body convulsed, and the white light grew brighter, surrounding me. Lightning? No, not quite. This was a slow-building light, one that seemed to spread over me like the rising sun. There were figures in the light, beckoning, beckoning...

*I seek time,* I thought, feeling myself being pulled to the light.

*I can give you time, my friend. I can give you time in spades. Now, will you go to the light, or come to me?*

## 14.

It is with no regret that I found it within me to push myself up with both hands. It is with no regret that the golden light above me faded into the distance. And it is with no regret that I understand—nay, that I know—I will never, ever see that light again.

And, yes. I did say nay.

I am, after all, over five hundred years old.

How I found my feet, I do not know. How I placed one foot in front of the other, I do not know that either. But somehow, some way, I forged ahead, through the rain, up a muddy trail, and finally along a winding, exterior stairway with, undoubtedly, glorious views of the vale below. But it was night, and it was raining, and I dared not look at anything other than the next stone step before me.

Up I went, up and around and through the driving wind and lashing rain, moving steadily, inexorably toward my own salvation. This was my heaven. This was my hell. My eternity awaited me at the top of these stairs... along with the man I had seen feasting upon the cat...

And so I climbed...

And climbed...

\*\*\*

He was waiting for me at the open door, but never did offer me a hand.

I'd asked him why later, and he had told me it was because he had to know I wanted this, that, beyond his offer for help, it had been me who pushed for this. I had asked why he cared, and he had opened his hands and smiled and said, "Because I have to live with myself forever, after all."

I would learn later that he was not like the others. Indeed, he was one who fought the entity within, who had gained dominion over the darkness within.

But then I had collapsed at his feet, and reached my arms out and said to him, "Help me. Please."

He had nodded, and his movement had been swift and terrible, and I found myself in his clutches, a searing pain in my neck, and my body completely immobile. Whether he had stunned me or whether I was in shock, I do not know. But I lay there on my side, my arms still reaching out, his face pressed into the crook of my neck, his hot breath on my skin, and felt what the alley cat must have felt. The sensation of being consumed.

But unlike the cat, I did not meet my demise.

There are those who think we die, Samantha Moon, when we become what we become. But they are mistaken, are they not? Are you not more alive than ever? Are you not stronger, and more powerful than you could ever imagine? The physical body certainly goes through a major shift, but it does not die, as you well know. Although the physical body now must accommodate something darker and often evil, it also must accommodate something else. Something that gives us our true immortality, something not often written about, or even known to most of our kind. But I will tell you now, although this might be information you have gleaned yourself. After all, I have seen firsthand how inquisitive you can be.

The body, in fact, becomes a receptacle for the soul itself, Sam. That is why there is no heaven for us. And if the "no heaven" part is news to you, then I am sorry to break it to you now, in this manner. But it is the truth. The soul is drawn from the energetic realm and summoned into these physical bodies, which, sadly, are still susceptible to physical death, under certain conditions, despite our kinds' ability to live forever. The forever part comes with a caveat. We cannot be burned alive, suffer silver to the heart, or survive a beheading, although I know of one such man who had. A horseman, in fact. There was, as you might recall, a famous book written about him. Truth disguised as fiction.

But I digress...

Indeed, it is the full power of the soul, contained in these clumsy bodies, that gives us our immortality, Sam. Not the dark masters who worm their way in. True, these so-called masters have developed the magic necessary to draw the soul from heaven, but that is the extent of their power. Every good thing you do, every bit of joy you feel, is from your inner self, Sam. The darkness within you would lead you to believe otherwise. They would even lead you to believe that you must drink blood. No, Sam. It is *they* who crave the blood. Not you. Never believe their lies. Ever. Someday... yes, someday you will learn how to control even this craving; that is, if you desire it to be so. It is really dependent on how much of the darkness within has taken control. Alas, this is talk for another time.

Back to the stone manor. Back to his lips on my throat. And not just his lips. No, I could feel his teeth, his fangs, deep into my neck, destroying the flesh, the arteries, perhaps even some of the bone, too. Deeply, he drank, and I was helpless. I was also in a great deal of pain, although I found I could not utter a word, nor even a moan. Neither could I move a muscle. I was his helpless victim, although a victim I was not.

I knew little of vampires, or why he fed from me so ravenously. Only I knew something was happening, something great and important—something life-altering and life-giving.

No, I could not move a muscle, but tears of joy streamed down my face.

And I smiled within...

## 15.

The next few days were hell.

The confusion, the pain, the hunger, the shift from mortal to immortal as the entirety of my soul settled into this bulky physical husk. Despite the changes within, some often quite painful, I still felt better than I had for the previous months and even years. No longer did I feel death was imminent. Quite the opposite. Now, I felt as if, yes, as if there was a chance I would make it through another week. And another week was all I asked. Just a few more days to find the Red Rider.

But as I lay holed up in the home, near a shuttered window kept closed during the day, I began to suspect I was going to have more than one week. Or two weeks. As I felt the change come over me, as I hallucinated and shuddered and briefly fought the thing that I knew had gained access to me—the thing I saw lurking in my mind, watching me—I could feel my body growing stronger. I had been so weak, so close to death, that any improvement would have been pronounced. Indeed, even in those first few hours, it quickly became apparent that I had shifted from dying... to actually growing stronger. Each hour, stronger and stronger, even as I was left shuddering and sweating and naturally resisting the darkness that sought purchase within me.

Perhaps I was more willing than some, and so my conversion was not as dramatic as others. I suspect yours had been confusing and terrible. How often I wanted to come to your side at the hospital and ease you through the transition, to explain to you what was happening and why. But I knew... ah, I knew you had gone through enough. And who was I, after all? Just your father from many lifetimes ago... a man you had no memory of. Who was I to comfort you, when, in fact, it had been I who had stolen heaven away from you?

Perhaps I should have let you die in my arms that night, six years ago (well, six years, as of the writing of this letter). But how... could I? True, you would have been reborn again, and I would have found you again, I hope. I don't always find you, Sam Moon, but I have learned to follow your soul's imprint. It is no easy task and it took me decades to understand how to understand such energies. But where there is a will, there is a way. If I can teach you anything, let it be that. The Universe will bring you an answer, always. In this case, it brought to me a master's master who taught me to go deeper within myself, so deep, in fact, that I stood outside myself, in a place where I could see the energies coming and going to the earth. The master's master called this the Winter Wind, and I could see why. Mostly, I could see the new souls, eager for re-birth; I could also see the tired and beaten-down energies ready for the relief of death. It was here, in a state of deep meditation, that I observed your own re-birth, over and over. Including your birth into this present life.

Those who live and die leave a celestial imprint. However, those who are immortal—that is, those who are permanently connected to the earth—are beyond my sight, and that's a damn shame.

But I am getting ahead of myself.

In those early days of my transformation, I was taught much by my own vampire sire. First and foremost, despite the severity of my attack, he was a gentle man, one who had gained dominion over his own dark master by feasting only upon the animals, thus depriving his dark master of the nutrients it needed to take him over. I learned from him and kept my own monster at bay, all these years. Truth be known, my own dark master has long since grown quiet. I suspect he is in a state of stasis, awaiting the moment of my death to be free again and seek a more willing partner.

Or not. Perhaps I have taken the fight out of him and he seeks only release. His release will not come, ever... unless, I, too, die.

And so the weeks passed into months and I grew more comfortable in my new skin. I was shown tricks and techniques, all of which I have utilized to great effects... even while learning even more about my talents. I learned to teleport, which I hope I have passed on to you. As your sire, I have passed along some of my own talents. Bear in mind, you are the result of a heady mixture of talents, Samantha Moon: my own, your dark master's, your latent witchy abilities, and, most prevalent, your own soul.

As the months piled on, I was eager to set out in search of the Red Rider. I was a new man, after all. More powerful than I'd ever been before—or could ever imagine. My own sire was sad to see me leave, for I had provided him much company in our time together. My education consisted of learning of the dark masters, the other magical creatures of this world, of heaven and hell and the devil, of demons and angels and our place in the world. I would learn that this was my heaven, and to make the most of my time here. I was taught that once I died, I would be reabsorbed back into the Source of All That Is, but that it was nothing to fear. I believed him, and I still believe him. He was, after all, one of the original vampires.

But, alas, it was time for me to leave the still-youngish-looking man, who, I would learn, was over a hundred years old. I was told that I looked like a healthy old man now. Healthy and vibrant and pale as could be. Vampirism doesn't reverse age, I would learn, although it had given me new life and strength in abundance. Still, I was told I might just be one of the oldest-looking vampires in the world, and that gives me a chuckle. After all, someone has to be the oldest, right?

The key was, I didn't feel old. I felt powerful and ready to take on the world. Or, in the least, to find the Red Rider. To find him and kill him. Whatever the hell he was. Then again, I wasn't entirely sure what the hell I was either.

And so I set off again, a changed man, a vampire, but always, first, a father.

A father hell-bent on revenge.

## 16.

I looked up from the scroll, knowing there were but a few paragraphs left.

I used my phone and coffee mug as weights to keep the thing from rolling back into itself, and sat back and rubbed my eyes. Truth was, my eyes felt perfect. Never had they felt better. For that matter, never had all of me felt better, either. No aches and pains. No kinks or flare-ups. Just a perfectly functioning system, all thanks to dark magicks... and my own soul.

Lots was going on in this five-foot-three-inch frame.

I'm not a fast reader and a half hour or more had passed. I had paused often and reflected and re-read scenes, soaking them in, acknowledging them, and working through them emotionally.

Those re-born throughout time would, of course, have many fathers. That should be of no surprise. That one of my fathers had given up heaven to find my killer was new to me, and a bit overwhelming, too. Certainly, I had no memory of the life of which he spoke. It was, what, 400 years ago? In Europe, no less.

He'd heard me scream and went running after me, only to discover the horse, rider and me had disappeared into thin air.

He'd searched for me for months after, only to find my discarded body in a pit of other such discarded bodies. I could not imagine the filth of that pit, the stink, the horror of finding your own child atop it. He had not gone into detail about the exact condition of my body, but I suspected, based on his other choice words, that he had found me partially consumed. Or perhaps more than partially. Maybe damn near completely. But he had known it was me, and had buried me, and then, he had spent the rest of his human life hunting for the "elusive" Red Rider, a name he had given the man based on the cloak he had worn.

And when he had finally come to the end of his existence, he had sought out what he believed to be a vampire. And as death approached, he was re-born again as a vampire, only to continue his search... up to just a few years ago. That was when, of course, Rand the Vampire Hunter had ended my father's search for justice.

Of course, I use the word "father" liberally here. Perhaps even loosely. I am taking a dead vampire's word that this was all true. That he had been taught by a master's master to seek me out in the heavens, and that he had watched over me, life after life, protecting me down through the ages. That he had, in fact, turned me only to save me.

"I need a drink," I whispered.

Although alcohol had no effect on me, I poured a glass of wine anyway and returned to my study, sipping it, enjoying what I could from it, since my taste buds were mostly dead. Still, I caught a hint of the stuff, and that was enough. Or, rather, it had to be enough.

I moved aside my placeholder phone and pressed the rolled parchment flat, and resumed reading...

\*\*\*

I would spend many centuries looking for this animal.

Always, I was a step behind, or a mile behind, or months behind. Rarely did I even catch sight of him, but always did I see the destruction he caused in his wake. The distraught families, the wailing mothers, the villages all looking for a missing girl, not realizing she was not only long gone, but that she was, perhaps even at that moment, being consumed by he who once called himself a priest, but was now so very far from God that he might as well have been the devil's right-hand man.

Maybe he was.

How did he do it? I would learn through many inquiries and my own deduction that the bastard was able to hone in on the most magical. Those with latent abilities, or budding abilities, were of no interest to him; at least, not in this lifetime. Later, as their magic blossomed, so too did their chances of befalling a fate worse than death.

Over the centuries, I would learn more about him. I would discover that he knew I was on to him, and he took extra precautions to throw me off his trails. Sadly, I never knew when he would strike next, and always, I was too late. Never was I able to save those he stalked, for I never knew who might be his next victim.

That is, until I had heard of a girl locked away in a dungeon, a girl the locals had proclaimed to be a real witch, and a nasty one at that. After all, who else was to blame for the pestilence and plague, the disease and sickness, the foul weather and ruined crops? A witch, of course. Personally, I always thought witches had better things to do than to summon bad weather or chicken pox. After all, I'd seen *you* at work, dear one. I had witnessed first-hand your sweet and beautiful connection to the world around you. Never could I imagine you bringing hellfire upon the crops of your neighbors, even if they had it coming to them.

Then again, perhaps I was spoiled by you.

And so I sought out this witch; after all, if she was as powerful as I believed, surely she would be of interest to the Red Rider.

By now, I had spent many decades being what I am, and it was without incident that I located her in prison, subdued the guards with a few simple suggestions, and snapped open her lock. Immediately, I could see I was dealing with the real deal. She sat upon a nearby bench, surrounded by rats and mice and insects, all of which swarmed over her, through her clothing and hair, and up and down her arms and legs, all while she giggled and spoke to them, ignoring me completely.

When she finally acknowledged me, I was immediately struck by the power of her gaze. A gaze that reminded me so much of your own. Penetrating, calculating and wise. But that was where the similarities ended. First, she was no girl, easily going on thirty. Next, she was tall and robust, sporting thick arms and squarish hands. Her neck and jowls shook and her ruddy skin radiated health and vitality. Her brown hair was long and straight, and I was instantly smitten.

She knew me for what I was before I could think of what to say. I merely nodded, acknowledging her knowing observation, and she shrugged and smiled and turned back to her swarming friends. She smiled at them and said, "Go home, my friends," and in a blink, her creepy-crawly companions were gone in a scurry of feet, tails, and crackling exoskeletal armor.

She stood and I think I might have involuntarily stepped forward, so powerful was the force of my attraction. There was something unseen but felt around her, and I knew that this woman could not be contained by these bars. No, she had been *waiting* for me. We stood staring at one another, a witch and a vampire, while the guards slept contentedly outside, and it was of great relief that I saw in her eye a similar yearning, and we came forward together, as one, embraced and locked lips for an unknowable amount of time. And that is all I will say of our physical attraction. You are my child, after all, even if several hundred years removed.

Our whirlwind romance began, which was a much-needed reprieve and greatly appreciated. I'd been alone for so long, child. So very long. Her name was Millie, and we were a powerful force, indeed. She took up my cause, helping to search for Red Rider, even offering herself as bait, but never did he show in her lifetime, although we continuously found evidence of his destruction.

She would die in my arms a half-century later, and I miss her every day of my life. Never would I find love again, but I am okay with that, Sam. I had your mother, I had you, and I had Millie. A man should be so lucky.

I suspected Millie's power was both a beacon and a warning to avoid. She was, after all, a very,

very powerful witch. Unfortunately, not even her magicks could find the man, let alone capture him. But I would learn much in our time. I would learn that he feared fully matured witches. His preference was for the young and mostly helpless. He avoided people at all costs, and seemed uncannily adept at detecting traps.

And so I continued my search, alone.

\*\*\*

Like my sire, I refused the blood of man, and kept my dark master weak and forgotten.

Ultimately, I suspect I was not of much use to the dark masters' grand plan. After all, I had my own agenda and had little use of their silly war. Yes, I'd heard much about it from my sire, and also from others of my kind that I'd happened upon, including the various were-beasts. Yes, I did say various. Perhaps you have been made aware by now that our world is inhabited by many such magical creatures, all of whom are the result of the dark masters' dark influence. No, there was no rift in time and space. There was no opening from our world into the next. The creatures in our world are abominations, Sam, plain and simple. *We* are an abomination, too. We are the result of carefully calculated dark magic, magic so strong as to yank our souls from heaven, and "permanently" encase them here. I put *permanently* in quotes for good reason. That said, with luck—and with a lack of enemies—yes, some of us might see the end of days of this planet. Some of us might even see the sun extinguish and the earth grow cold. Some, not all. Very few, in fact.

And so the years piled on. As did the decades and centuries. Never did I feed upon a living human. Even when I turned you, I did not feed on you. No... I fed you. With my own blood.

Needless to say, I have made no progress in my hunt for the Red Rider. I know he is here in America, and has been for the past hundred years, hence my own presence. There is a new wave of witchcraft sweeping the land, and I know why. It is, quite literally, thanks to him. He'd extinguished so many magical lives that it took many generations for the magic to re-establish itself, so to speak, to take hold again, to grow again, to flourish again. It might also explain why I had not seen nor heard of him for nearly seventy years. I suspect he'd gone underground, dormant. Perhaps he was in a sort of hibernation mode. In fact, I had truly thought him dead; that is, until the disappearances started again. And they started back in the 1930s. Parents, do you want to know what happened to your children? More than likely, some of them expressed some form of magic. Perhaps even a lot of magic. Perhaps you laughed it off. Perhaps you ignored it. Or perhaps you were afraid of it. But with each charm, each incantation, each expression of magic, your child drew the Red Rider closer.

And then, your children were gone. Just like that. He appeared, snatched them away, and disappeared again, all while whole communities searched for evidence of them, only to find nothing. Want to know where to look? Look deep in the local caves. There, you will find your missing children, partially consumed, like you, dear Samantha.

I am sorry to be the bearer of bad news. But look no further than him. He is often the culprit.

Which brings me to almost the present.

You hadn't been re-born in many decades, and I was worried about that, too. Where do you go between lives, you might ask? Ah, I've seen a glimpse of that, too, in my meditative place there in the heavens, where I can see the comings and goings of all souls. A nice trick, really. If I survive the hunter's attack, perhaps I will destroy this letter and explain all to you in person, including many of the tricks I have learned. There is a world of pure energy, Sam, although you wouldn't see it as energy once in it. Indeed, it wouldn't look very different than the physical world. But it is there, and it is very, very different. I have seen only glimpses of it, but it is enough to know that I have given up something very beautiful indeed in my search for the Red Rider. Likewise, I have stolen it from you as well. I feel the pang of regret every day, even though I know in my heart I saved you from certain death. Perhaps I should have let you move on into the afterlife, to be re-born again, stronger than ever. Perhaps. But I also knew that the stronger you were, the more likely you would have attracted the Red Rider, and the vicious cycle would have started all over again. Then again, perhaps I would have captured the Red Rider by then. Perhaps.

Sam... many thoughts had gone through my mind as you lay in my arms, bleeding and dying. It is no great surprise to you that you would have died in minutes, if that. Your throat was torn open. Blood was pumping into the grass around us, soaking into the dirt.

But as I held you... ah, the tears. They spring forth even now. Hang on, child.

Okay, back again. I am jumping ahead of myself again. Let me backtrack a smidge.

After nearly sixty years since your last death—you finally appeared again. With the help of the master's master, I've been locked onto your soul signature for quite some time. Think of it as a tracking device. Sometimes—not always—in my meditative state, I caught sight of you in the world of energy. Playing and laughing and exploring the cosmos. These flashes of insight always made me smile, and, conversely, weep. The weeping always jerked me out of the meditation, which was fine. I knew you were safe in the world of energy, and I was content.

Ah, but thirty years ago, deep in my meditation, I found you elsewhere. I found you in a womb in northern California, and I literally pulled up shop and headed there right away. Your parents were... interesting, and I couldn't help but be jealous of the time they spent with my little girl, but it is what it is, and I had long since accepted that you would never remember, which was fine. Is fine. I was not here to reconnect with you. No, I was here—I existed—to kill the Red Rider, plain and simple. But if I could catch a glimpse of you... oh, it would lift my spirits up and keep me ever vigilant. As you can imagine, after so many years of failure, my hopes of catching the Red Rider have dimmed. But seeing you reborn again, alive and well, healthy and cooing and laughing and playing, ah... my spirits were lifted high indeed and my determination renewed.

I kept watch over you from a distance. In my meditative state, I could find you anywhere, particularly in the physical; that is, here on earth. Want to know a curious fact? Oh, you do? Sorry, it is my lame attempt at playfulness. Okay, here is the curious tidbit. In one of your lives, you were not even born on Earth. Once, you were born on a planet inhabited by what I could only call dragons. There, you were one of these beautiful creatures, flying lazily, contemplating life, and mating with another such creature. A beautiful, epic, brilliant, powerful creature in his own right. Interestingly, I sense him in you, somehow... a connection that has not yet been broken. Perhaps you sense him, too.

Perhaps not. Either way, he is there... watching.

Moving on. While watching you from afar, I continued my search for the Red Rider. Twice in the last twenty years, I caught sight of him. Both times, he was leaving his cave of choice, somehow aware that I was on to him. He is a fiercely magical being by this point, Sam. Perhaps the most magical of all. Had he wanted to, I suspect he could do away with me, but he has chosen not to. I suspect he is a coward, Sam, unwilling to fight another man at full strength. Rather, he would prey on the magical children of the world.

That said, I believe he tipped off the hunter who, even now, is stalking me. I sense the man nearby. I can see him, feel him. The hunters are a strange breed, Sam. They are skilled at remaining mostly undetected, especially by those of our kind. Only, our own inner warning system can detect them. Trust you me, mine has been going off continuously these past three months. Even now, as I write these words, my inner alarm is pinging softly just inside my inner ear. He is near. I can feel him. It is why I hastened to write this letter.

Yes, the Red Rider is as magical as they come, but he needs magic to live, too. I believe he uses it up, depletes it. That is when he is the weakest, between victims. It is not much to go on, but it is something. No, I am not asking you to take up my mantle, for, in many ways, this has been a fool's quest. How many years have I wasted in my pursuit? Hundreds, Sam. I've wasted many, many lifetimes.

That said, this abomination cannot be permitted to live. How many more mothers and fathers need to suffer before this thing is destroyed?

Okay, I am calm again.

And so I watched you grow into a beautiful woman. I watched you also brilliantly adapt to these modern times. Your past two lives, in particular, you worked as a nurse, sometimes using your latent magical skills to aid you, although you whispered nothing to anyone. At times, I suspected, you even doubted your own skills. And yet, they were there, when needed. How do I know this? I watched, Sam. I observed from afar, and sometimes, up close. Sometimes, yes, sometimes I even dipped into your mind. I'm sorry for such intrusions. I am but a lost and hurting father.

Once I saw you put down roots in Fullerton, I did the same, in a home that—if you are reading this letter—is all yours. I was pleased to watch your success, both in finishing graduate school and landing a job well suited to your skills and intellect.

I noted, however, that you hadn't come into your own just yet with magic. That was okay with me, truth be known. I was fine with that. That kept the Red Rider at bay. That said, I sensed the magic in you, and so did you if you were honest with yourself. So did the witchy trifecta, of which you were to be a part. How do I know this? Because one of them watched over you, as did I. She was in spirit, choosing not to be re-born during this cycle. She thought, perhaps correctly, that the trifecta might be better served having one of their members steadfastly within the world of energy. An odd concept, but one that could give them even more power, even if her magic was limited or nonexistent. It would put more pressure, surely on the other two members. But her broad-range knowledge should have proved invaluable. Again, how did I know this? I have lived a long time, Sam. And I am a bit of a detective myself, at this point. I can put two and two together and come up with a valid supposition.

So I waited, knowing something special was coming your way, knowing the full expression of magic was coming your way, too. You were a late bloomer, so to speak. Yes, it took all these lifetimes to get you back to full power after it had been stolen from you.

I watched your new family take shape, and I was pleased. You loved Danny, and I liked him, too. Well, up until a few years ago. But that is another story. You seem to be catching on to the bastard, and so I will not have to step in. Trust me, Sam Moon, it was all I could do to not show up at his work and put the fear of God in him. Or the fear of me in him.

As happy as I was to see you thriving and blossoming and your family growing, I found myself hurting all the more. Oh, how I wanted to be a part of your family! The eccentric grandfather who could perform real magic tricks for his grandkids, even if they were many lifetimes removed. Indeed, how much longer could I do this to myself? How much longer could I hurt and hunt? I didn't know. At times, I looked forward to death. For then, I would finally find peace, even if it meant losing all of myself back into the One Source, back into the One Mind. Even if it meant never existing again. Your life was on the right track. Peace had come to you, even if your own job was far from peaceful because I knew you could handle yourself.

And that's when the whispering occurred.

That's when my own dark master stirred within me.

The dark masters, it would seem, had long since been aware of you... and were waiting, so to speak. Waiting for their chance to pounce. I knew this because my own dark master gave me warning. You were exactly what they needed: an entity with a witchy heritage, born into an alchemical bloodline, which you happened to be in this lifetime. This was news to me. This I did not know.

Oh, they waited a long, long time for someone like you.

Apparently, witchy abilities can be sensed by more than just the Red Rider. Apparently, those born in the Hermetical bloodline have a signature in their aura: a silver serpent that wends its way in and out, in and out, over and around. The alchemists are aware of those in their bloodline, and have sought to mute the silver serpent with charms. But not all charms work all the time. Sometimes, charms are removed from a body. Sometimes, the silver serpent is free to be seen by any with eyes to see.

But here is another secret, Sam. The dark masters are also aware of the alchemical bloodlines. They keep tabs on them, and watch those they can, waiting for The One, so to speak. That is, she or he born with powerful magicks, and also born into the Hermetical bloodline.

Sam, it is safe to say you were marked for quite some time. All of which was unknown to me at the time, although I know it now.

And so the dark masters fed my own dark master, whom they knew to be weakened and even friendly toward me, false information, if you will.

I was led on a wild goose chase, thinking an attack was coming from elsewhere in the city, which was when you were jostled from sleep, and given the idea to go for a midnight run.

A midnight run? Really, Samantha.

Who jostled you? None other than your own dark master, Elizabeth. She'd been keeping an eye on you for some time, too, sometimes frightening you, although she never intended to scare you. Still, the proximity of her presence was enough to terrify you. How was it that she escaped the Void long enough to visit you in spirit? You will have to ask her. She was—and is—a dark master of the highest order. She undoubtedly has a few more tricks up her sleeve.

By the time I'd realized we had been duped, your attack was well under way. I immediately sought you out, honing in on you as I'm always able to do. Seeing you in my mind's eye, I teleported instantly to your side.

## 17.

There is another twist in the tale, as they say.

There is a reason I could not—would not—allow the vampire to turn you. There is a reason why, in fact, I drove a silver dagger deep into the vampire's heart, even while he hovered over you, ready to feed you from his own slit wrist.

First off, the dark masters have done a number on us.

Not only do they not tell us that the primary source of our powers—our strength, telepathy, teleportation, transformations, warning bells, you name it—all come from our own inner beings, but they have neglected to tell us something else entirely. You see, Sam—and I do apologize for taking your name so informally... it just feels right to my ear—but you see, something else happens when a vampire infects a mortal with his tainted blood.

There is, in fact, quite a lot that goes on, as you will see...

The instant the infection occurs, the soul is snatched from heaven, even while the dark master invades the unsuspecting victim, attaching itself, quite literally, for eternity. But something else happens, too. Something rarely talked about and rarely known, but of paramount importance to the dark masters.

It is a secondary entry point, a secondary back channel to access your thoughts and control you, an entry point that I effectively plugged up by turning you myself, rather than the monster they'd sent to attack you.

You see, Sam, when a vampire's blood irreversibly infects a human, a pathway of sorts is created, a connection, a link between sire and victim. The link, quite simply, allows me access to your mind itself.

Such access is terribly invasive, and it was why I had to turn you at all costs, and not the wretched beast who would have done so otherwise.

Sam, I know this is a lot to take in. It is why I did not approach you sooner. How could I have been able to get you to understand? Surely, you needed experience as a new vampire to understand what you were, years to control what you are. I was willing to give you this time, and approach you accordingly. I had not expected the hunter to disrupt my plans. Truly, I had envisioned giving you these words in person, perhaps high up on my balcony, as we gaze at the stars together. Yes, I harbor such idealistic visions. I have more, too, each more embarrassing than the next. But in all of them, we are together again, father and daughter, and life is as it should be and I am finally, finally content. Perhaps those days will still come. After all, should I survive the hunter's attack, you may never see these words. If so, maybe, just maybe we might still have that moonlit stroll along, say, a beach of your choice, talking the way only family can, laughing and telling stories.

Do you see how pathetic I am, Sam?

Still, these hopes and dreams are what drive me forward, along with the much darker and bleaker task of eliminating the Red Rider. But enough of him. Let's talk about our link.

Yes, we have a link, and we've had it the instant my blood trickled beyond your parted lips and down your damaged throat. We had it the moment the dark shadow appeared as if from the ground itself. I caught sight of a female with red eyes and long claws, something that had been very far removed from human, something that I suspected had been entombed in The Void for centuries perhaps. Later, I would learn just who found her way into you, and I would regret over and over again for having turned my baby girl into a monster like me. But there is literally no turning back now.

That is not quite accurate. I do have such a tool that could turn you back. I removed it from the man who attacked you and have since verified its veracity. It's a medallion. A ruby medallion, which I am certain will reverse vampirism. You see, I know curses and have seen magic, and I could feel the power of the medallion. How it works, exactly, I do not know. But I suspect it does have the power to reverse vampirism. If so, you can expect to find it with my belongings. It is, perhaps, the most precious gift I can give you. No, I will not use it on myself. It is for you, dear heart. You, and you alone.

The link. Yes, the link.

From the moment your soul was summoned from the heavens, you went from mortal, to immortal, and a pathway was opened in my mind. A pathway that led directly to your mind.

Not telepathy, child. This is a real opening, a real neural network that I can access at any given moment. Let's see, I will access it now...

There you are, pacing your home, awaiting the sun to sink below the horizon. You are anxious, jittery. Do not worry, little one, the anxiousness will leave over time, and you will flow more naturally with circadian rhythms of the sun and moon. For now, though, you are anxious and so I will give you a small prompting that all will be okay. Okay, I just did so and you, of course, believe it to be your own thought, and so you are sitting now on your couch. But your worry has not left. Instead, you wonder why your husband is late again and why he keeps talking about his secretary. I ease your mind of all that as well. *Relax child*, I tell you from deep in your mind, and now you are taking a deep breath, relaxing, telling yourself that everything will work out, somehow. Somehow.

*Somehow.*

And now you are crying, but I let you cry. Sometimes a good cry is needed. So much is built up inside you, child. So much pain and worry that I sit here now, shaking my head, worried for you, but loving you all the more.

Do you see now why I couldn't allow that monster inside your brain, why I could not allow him to exert such control over you, even if such control was in the form of mild suggestions? Should I die, that opening will be forever closed, and that's not such a bad thing, is it? I do not pry into your life, but sometimes I cannot help a small peek, and I watch from afar, laughing when you laugh, struggling when you struggle, and hungering when you hunger. In those moments our minds are truly one. Perhaps, at times, you have gotten a hint of an old man in an old house, obsessed with you and the Red Rider. The opening is not as strong in the other direction, meaning from you to me. Think of a funnel. I can see you, bright and bigger than life. I am but a pinprick in your own thoughts, easy to ignore and dismiss. Luckily, you do not question your very thoughts, and for that I am grateful. It shows me that I am not too intrusive, although I do feel guilty for watching you as much as I do.

So there you have it, child. My story. My reason for existing. The reason you are what you are. The reason heaven has been stolen from you. I take full blame for that. I could have watched you die in my arms. I did not have to turn you. That was all me, and I have only myself to blame for that.

But please remember: although there is no heaven for you, you can make heaven on earth. There is beauty all around you, and many hundreds and hundreds of years in front of you. The world has plenty to enjoy, even for the undead. And always there is something to learn, about both yourself and the world around you. So much to learn.

With that said, if you are reading these words, it means I am long dead, by about six years at least, enough time for my own bloodsucking attorney to certify that there will be no returning for me.

What are my parting words for you, Samantha Moon? Would you like to know what we named you four hundred years ago? Would you like to know what I called you when you were my little one? Oh, you do? Daisy. You were my sweet little Daisy, and you loved flowers so much. You never picked them, no. You would smell them and touch them and dance around them.

My sweet little Daisy. You are all grown up.

I wish you a long life, dear heart. I wish you to

never take any moment for granted. I wish each new day brings you love and joy. There are worlds beyond this, Sam Moon. You have lived in one of them. But there are also lives beyond the ones you know now. Allow for those you love to grow old and live their lives. Do not be tempted to change them. Allow the natural progression as God intended. There will be more children, even if they are not your own, more friends, more lovers, more dreams and desires. Never forget who you are, and do not hate anyone or anything, even the thing within you. Over time, she will soften, you will see. Yes, I have long since implanted within you the need to drink only animal blood, and yes, the entity within you hates me for that. But she can hate me. Weirdly, strangely, perversely, I love her too. After all, if not for her and others like her, a loophole would not have been found in the system, and they would not have been able to find their way back to earth, and she would not have been able to give you eternal life. You live because of these dark masters, Sam. They are truly evil geniuses. Learn to work with them, not hate them, and you will see the rough seas begin to smooth.

If you are reading these words, it is also likely the Red Rider lives on, killing the magical among us. I am not asking you to take up my mantle. But should you find yourself in the vicinity of the Red Rider, please do not hesitate to blot the earth of this disease.

With that, I leave you with love and smiles. I see the sun has set and you are calm now in your home. I like seeing you calm. God bless you, little one.

## 18.

I found myself crying harder than I expected to, and it took me many minutes to get the tears under control. That a man had given up everything for me, my one-time father... oh, geez.

More tears flowed and, at one point, Anthony was hugging me while Tammy stood in the doorway. She had, undoubtedly, read every word with me, seeing it through my eyes. My daughter was, of course, the ultimate snoop. In this case, although the letter was deeply personal, I did not mind that she had seen what I had seen.

"It's okay, Mommy," Anthony was saying, over and over, sounding much younger than his fifteen years.

Tammy said nothing, but I saw the tears in her own eyes. She was wearing sweats and a Supergirl shirt. I'd asked earlier what the difference was between the Supergirl and Superman logo was, and, with a full eye roll that surely hurt, informed me that there was no difference. Duh. And added, "You're such a dork."

"Well, it's a legitimate question," I had asked. "Like, legit."

"Did mom just say 'legit'?" Anthony had asked, sauntering by with a sandwich in hand. Correction, three sandwiches in hand, all smashed together. Jelly and mayo oozed between slices of bologna, peanut butter and bananas. Sweet Moses, I had not just seen that.

The memory comes and goes as she stood in the doorway, crying quietly herself. She knew everything I knew about my own sire. I asked if she was okay, and she nodded, wiped her eyes, and asked if I was okay. I answered honestly. *I didn't know.*

Anthony never did ask what was wrong. But when he saw that his work here was done, that his mother was under some semblance of control, he headed back into the living room, and continued his video game.

I carefully rolled up the scroll and re-tied the leather strap. I opened the top drawer in my desk and set it in inside, just behind my pens. The scroll was, quite literally, the story of a life. An important life. Jeffcock, despite how outrageous the name was, had been my father. A very good father at that. A loving and kind and hardworking father who let a little girl enjoy the magic of the world, without judgment or punishment, a father who had seen his world get turned upside down.

The scroll was also another story. It was the story of me, as a young girl, in another world and another time. It was a story I knew I would re-read over and over again, especially the scenes of playing in the woods, connecting with nature, and of me happy and content, pure and full of joy. I wonder... yes, I wonder if I would ever be that happy again? I doubted it. I had been magical and alive and connected, and all was right in the world.

Until the Red Rider appeared and took me away.

And he didn't just take me away, did he? A part of me suspects I had been consumed alive, one bite at a time. By the world's greatest monster.

The greatest monster of all.

Well, fuck him and the devil horse he rode in on.

I was going to find him, and I was going to destroy him. I was going to continue my father's search, whether he wanted me to or not.

And I suspected he did.

I had once been a federal agent, but I was a different kind of agent now, wasn't I?

Indeed. I was an agent for the Angel of Death.
And I had The Devil Killer.
The sword of all swords.
Fuck the Red Rider.

I was coming for him.

# 19.

I needed to clear my head, which was why I was boxing.

These days, Jacky only emerged from his back office to watch me spar or hit the heavy bag. Rarely did he speak, although he mumbled to himself, with the occasional, "Keep your hands up" outburst. A quick dip into his mind revealed confusion and chaos and a love for boxing, exactly in that order. His love for the sport gave him clarity. While in there (his head, that is), I did a little maintenance. I walled up some static, chaotic thoughts that I knew to be associated with dementia, brought on by real brain trauma from years of fighting. Decades, actually. I also gave him a gentle suggestion that all was well.

Once done, he spoke a little clearer and sometimes walked over to me and other boxers and showed them how to deliver a quick jab, of which he did expertly. Sadly, the dark aura around him had grown since the last time I'd seen him. But not wildly so, which meant he still had some time here on the planet, although not a lot of it.

He mostly remembered my name, although sometimes he called me Sal and asked how the old gang was. I dipped into his brain and saw a group of Irish ruffians patrolling a street corner. Not a real gang. In fact, they were the opposite. They were there to keep the streets safe from the real gangs. And there was a much younger Jacky, full of spunk and spit, ready to take on all comers, afraid of no one and nothing. Sal, I saw, had been his good friend... a friend who had died decades ago, according to a flashing, fleeting memory. I told Jacky the old gang was good, keeping the streets safe, and that he owed me a dinner. Yeah, I saw that in his memory too... a dinner gone unpaid to Sal, a dinner Jacky regretted never paying up on. Jacky had smiled and wiped his tears, then shook his head, blinked, and seemed to come back to his senses.

"Hands up, Sam!"

"Yes, sir."

At present, Jacky had gone back to his office and I was shadowboxing alone when a real shadow emerged from the floor and rose up before me. The shadow shifted and wavered and I realized it was little more than paper-thin. I paused and dropped my hands. Sweat poured off me, which was undoubtedly a credit to the sheer amount of water I drank. Undead or not, immortal or not, a body needed freakin' water. Cells needed water. Everything needed water. No, I didn't crave water, but I gave it water, whether it wanted it or not.

The amorphous shadow took on some shape, but not a lot of it. It had once been humanoid. Maybe. It wasn't a ghost either, as its body was not composed of the electrified static energy that I see everywhere, the energy that ghosts can draw to themselves to give shape. No, this was not a ghost nor anything I was familiar with. The red eyes, of course, I had seen before. At the home of my sire... my one-time father. Was it one of the entities I'd seen crawling over the walls of his home and hiding in its shadows, those entities that fled from the floating candelabras? I didn't know, but it looked damned close.

Whatever it was, it hovered a few inches from the ground, its red eyes unblinking. Had I not been so tough, I might have run in terror. But I'd fought the devil, his demons, and his three-headed dog. A strange shadow with glowing red eyes put only a small amount of fear in me.

"What are you?" I asked, certain no one could overhear me.

Jacky's gym was big, occupying the bottom floor of one of Fullerton's oldest buildings, and I was in a far corner, alone. There had been a bank here once, I was told. It had also been nearly robbed, with both robbers being shot and killed, or so Jacky had told me. Interestingly, two spirits—both male, both wearing fedoras—often watched the ladies box. Unfortunately, whoever they were, they were little more than scattered energy, with only hints of their former selves. Their souls, their true souls, were long gone. These were nothing but memories. Still, enough of them were still here that I'd always meant to ask about their story. Were they just common robbers? Or were they part of a big Prohibition gang? I sensed their story was important, but I never knew why I sensed it. Luckily, they were always here.

"I am nothing," came a voice that was more felt than heard. Indeed, I could see the vibrations of the sound reverberate around it, emanating out like cracking waves.

"You are something, or I wouldn't be able to see or hear you." I lowered my voice and continued slowly bobbing and weaving, casually punching the air around me. The movements were mostly to cover the fact that I appeared to be talking to myself.

"I do not know what I am."

"Were you alive once?" I asked.

"I suspect so, which is why I often take this shape."

"What shape do you take other times?"

"No shape at all, Samantha Moon."

I paused in my sparring. "You know me?" I asked, my voice rising a little. Some heads turned my direction and I cracked my neck and shook out my arms and legs and mumbled some lame pep talk. The heads turned away as the shape drew closer, wavering and flapping on winds unseen and unfelt.

"You are the master's offspring."

"Kinda sorta," I said under my breath. I didn't think telepathic communication would work since I didn't think the thing in front of me had a head. "But yeah, close enough."

"The master is dead?"

"That, I can confirm."

The shadow wavered and rippled in front of me. Sometimes, his red eyes winked in and out of existence, then back again, and I realized, amazingly, the thing was blinking.

"He left my brothers and sisters bound to his home."

"And why were your brothers and sisters bound to his home? And what the hell does that even mean?"

But the thing didn't answer immediately, and I resumed shadow punching, picking up my pace, soon punching in a blur while a free standing, paper-thin poster of death fluttered and wavered nearby.

"I do not remember, Samantha Moon."

"But you remember my name."

"I only just heard it, but that, too, will soon be

forgotten."

"You have been dead a long time," I said.

"I suspect so."

"You never moved on to heaven or hell."

"No, Samantha Moon."

"Were you dark masters?"

"I... don't know. The concept feels familiar."

I nodded, wondering if these were one-time, low-level dark masters who'd escaped the devil upon death, and had been running ever since. Not all dark masters made it safely into the Void: take my own dumbass ex-husband for example.

"Why did the master bind your friends to his house, and how did you escape?"

The thing before me rose and fell on the currents of space, or non-space, and watched me for a long minute or so. I watched it watching me, wondering why the hell it would need to blink, and figuring it was probably only acting out a distant, perhaps forgotten memory.

It occurred to me then that I, Samantha Moon, lived in the cracks and fissures of space and time, those nooks and crannies that lie outside the standard cycles. So did this thing before me. So did Kingsley—who, by the way, I had a date with tonight. So did, really, everyone I knew. We were all outliers, strangers in a familiar land. I was just absorbing this revelation when the shadow spoke.

"He kept us safe. I recall him saying that. Yes, he said it once or twice. Or maybe more. He said he was keeping us safe from the fires of hell."

"Why does he keep enchanted candles in the house?" I asked under my breath, nodding at a woman who grabbed a spare yoga mat from nearby. She didn't smile back. A quick dip in her mind and... yup, she'd heard me talking to myself and thought I was a big weirdo. I encouraged her to forget I was even here and to not be so damn judgmental in the future. I wasn't sure how long that last suggestion would stick.

"We have a tendency to gravitate toward humans. We love humans. We want to... I dunno... be part of them, live with them, become one with them."

I nodded. "Possess them."

The thing nodded eagerly. "Yesss."

"But you've forgotten why or what your purpose here on earth was."

"We have forgotten most things, Samantha Moon."

"How did you escape the master's house?"

"His spell weakened over time. I am the strongest of my brothers and sisters. They were too afraid to break it, but I was not."

"What is it you want from me?" I asked. I nearly called it Thing #1.

"I seek the release of my brothers and sisters," he said.

"So that you may possess humans later? I don't think so."

The thing shook its head vigorously. "I do not know why I say these words, or what they really mean, but I know we are not ready to possess, nor can we possess. No, Samantha Moon, we seek release."

"And then what?"

"There is no 'then what,' There is only release."

I thought about the thing's request. I also considered why my one-time father had bound the entities. I said, "Go back to the home and I will consider your request."

"Very well."

"Wait. How did you find me?"

"I've been following you, ever since your departure."

"Okay, that's not creepy at all. Okay, go."

It said nothing, but bowed low, and kept on bowing until it had merged with the floor. I had only a brief flash of it moving off into the corners and up the wall and scurrying from wall to wall, until it found an air conditioning duct and disappeared.

I resumed shadow boxing, although the term had taken on a whole new meaning for me.

## 20.

Before my date with Kingsley, I had managed to pull together another meeting, one that had literally fallen into my lap. Sometimes a case—even a very strange case involving a witch killer that spanned centuries—caught a break. This was such a break.

Before heading to the gym, I'd reached out to a man of interest. A man I was certain I would not hear back from for many months. A man who wasn't just any man, but the man who had ended the life of my one-time father. Rand the vampire hunter was not only in Southern California, but he was free for a quick drink.

Which we were having now.

Like I said... a break.

I'd showered and changed at the gym's locker room and briefly wondered how I looked. Luckily, there was no one else in the locker room to catch sight—or *not* catch sight—of the freak who didn't show up in the oversized mirror. I assumed I looked presentable, shrugged, and headed out to Rockin Taco, literally next door to Jacky's gym. Like I said, sometimes I catch a break. I wasn't complaining.

A dueling piano bar might not be the first place one would imagine a vampire and a vampire hunter to meet. Then again, maybe it was the perfect place. Maybe the dueling nature of the pianos perfectly symbolized the dueling nature of my own love/hate relationship with Rand. Or maybe I just liked the cute piano players.

Indeed, as our drinks were served, the raucous crowd and energetic pianists (yes, I can hear Anthony laughing at that one), were having a great time. Although the brick walls looked like they might not survive the next earthquake, the massive wooden bar itself appeared to have been carved from a single giant redwood. How they got that sucker in here, I hadn't a clue. Maybe they'd built the bar *around* the fallen tree. It was a working theory.

Admittedly, I wasn't sure how I felt about Rand. Truth was—if that crazy scroll written by the crazy vampire was to be believed—he had ended the life of the man who had been my father 500 years ago. I should hate Rand. Hell, the man had almost ended my life, too. Amazingly, we had gone on to become friends, including an adventure in Europe that I didn't talk about much.

Anyway, Rand was as I remembered: blond-haired and hunky. My first memory of him had been, of course, when he had delivered the ruby medallion to my front door. I would learn later that it had been a sort of recon mission for him. At the time, I had only remembered him in his too-tight tan shorts, walking away from my house after delivering the package. There was a good chance I might have made a double-entendre joke or two about his package and signing the log. Not my best material, but at least I had entertained myself. Anyway, he had been impersonating a UPS driver at the time. Recon mission or not, he had delivered something very special to me. Something that, quite frankly, had saved the life of my son... and set my son on a path of no return, so to speak. My son, who had been briefly transformed into a vampire. My son, who had entertained his own dark master, even for just a short time. My son, who would grow into what could only be described as a superhero.

Says the woman sporting wing tattoos.

Tattoos that were oh-so-much more than tattoos.

And all because of Rand's special delivery that day. He didn't have to hand-deliver that ruby medallion, but he had... and had inadvertently set in motion a chain of events that had changed my life—and that of my son's life—forever.

Our drinks had just been delivered. Old-school Budweiser in the can for him and house zinfandel for me. Although my food ring is nice, I still feel mild discomfort when I stray too far from the vampiric basics, aside from blood. And the basics were white wine and water, both of which went down smooth, without a rumbling in the tummy, and I liked that.

Ring or no ring, the alcohol had no effect on me, which was sometimes a damned shame. I liked letting loose every now and then. A good buzz was... nice.

"First things first, Rand," I said. "Still hunting vampires?"

"I am."

"And how do you feel about a vampire sitting across from you now?"

"Kinda like those dueling pianists sitting across from each other."

"We're not dueling," I said. "At least, I don't think we are."

"No, we're not. But sitting with you now... goes against my nature."

"And what is your nature?" I asked.

He picked up his pale lager, took a sip. "It is hard to put into words, Sam."

"Try." I was admittedly curious after reading my one-time father's words on the subject.

"It is a... compulsion. How do you explain a compulsion?"

"You're doing fine. Keep going."

"There is within me a need to give balance to

the world."

"What is out of balance?"

"The predators."

"Are there that many vampires?" I asked.

"It's not the amount of vampires, Sam. One vampire can alter the balance. One vampire can remain undetected for centuries. One vampire can, over time, ravage a population. A particularly skilled vampire keen on avoiding detection and with a taste for human blood and, worse, with a fascination for killing, is a nearly impossible enemy to kill for the average man."

"And you are not average?"

"Not quite, Sam."

"You were born into this."

He merely nodded and drank more beer. I could sense the silver on him. I could even sense the silver pumping in his blood. I could also sense the garlic, too, which lately had begun to nauseate me. In fact, I was pretty sure it was the reason my eyes were watering now.

"Was your father a hunter?" I asked.

"Yes. And so was my mother, and so is my daughter."

I remembered his daughter. "Now there's a female version of you out there hunting vampires?"

"No, Sam. She specializes in the were-creatures."

"Yikes. Should my friend be alarmed?"

"Your boyfriend," said Rand, correcting me,

"should be fine. After the, ah, incident with your own attacker, my family has, ah, shifted how we do business."

"Shifted how?"

"We only hunt *known* killers."

"You regret killing him?"

"In a word, yes."

Except I didn't sense that he really regretted killing my sire, or regretted killing anyone, quite frankly. I sensed within him a love for killing, but that could have been me projecting. No, I didn't enjoy killing. Elizabeth did, maybe. Not me. Still, there was something off about Rand. I asked about his family, and he told me a little more, not much. There were other hunters like him. Not many, but enough to keep the balance, enough to keep the vampires and werewolves and other such creatures in check. Most, like him, formed killing squads of mercenaries; that is, non-hunters. Meaning, these others were not born into the hunting trade. Rather, they enjoyed a steady paycheck, and killing the undead was as good a gig as any.

"Mind if we switch subjects, Sam? We only just sat down. Truth was, your sire, Mr. Jeffcock Letholdus, didn't deserve to die, and that was a lesson learned by me—and my family."

I nodded, repressing my own feelings. To know that the man who sat in front of me was responsible for ending the life of the amazing man who had fathered me and loved me over the centuries was...

hard to take. No, I didn't want to hurt him or attack him. Attempting both would invariably be the end of me. I knew Rand's reflexes were nearly as fast as my own, and the hunter was armed to the teeth. No, I wanted to hate him. I wanted to hate him and scream at him and beat on his chest and remind him what a bastard he was and what an amazing man J.C. had been, vampire or no vampire. But I didn't, although I did look away and wipe my eyes.

Luckily, the dueling pianos were drowning out most of this conversation, which was one of the reasons why I'd chosen Rockin' Taco. That, and maybe the cute piano players.

"Are you wearing garlic?" I asked.

"You are especially sensitive these days, Sam Moon," he said, and leaned forward and pulled out a bulbous necklace cluster. "Only three cloves."

"Well, you smell like garlic bread without the bread."

He chuckled lightly. "Sam, I was wearing the same amount of garlic on the night we met, and you didn't seem to mind."

He was right, and I hated that he was right. These days, garlic was affecting me, ever since I'd first noticed its effects in Richmond, Virginia... 150 years ago. Back then (yes, thanks, in large part, to the mother of all voodoo curses), I'd first been made aware of the effects of garlic when confronted with a whole ring of the stuff. Immediately, I'd noticed my system shutting down. I'd felt weaker, slower, and stunted. I'd also lost the ability to read minds. And that had been a whole ring of the stuff. This... this was just three damn cloves. Interestingly, I couldn't remember exactly where or when I had been confronted with the garlic. The memory was there, but the place and events surrounding it, weren't. Time travel was damn weird. Either way, since then, garlic posed some problems for me.

"I hit a nerve, I'm sorry," said Rand.

"It's not you, it's just that..."

"The garlic is affecting you more and more?"

"Yes."

"And you don't like that?"

"No."

"Because it means you are slipping more and more to the dark side?"

"If that's what it means, yes," I said.

He nodded. "Yes and no. But it does mean that you've been at this vampire game for a long time now."

"Eleven, twelve years."

"You've been undead for over a decade."

"Dead, undead. It's subjective."

"Can you read my mind, Sam?"

I blinked at the question... and tried to dip in. *Tried* being the operative word here. Although I sensed his thoughts, dipping in seemed, suddenly, a nearly impossible task. Maybe if I tried hard enough... except I didn't feel like trying harder. I felt like I wanted to... sleep.

"I can't. And I feel weird."

"You feel tired?"

"Yes. Is it the garlic?"

"That and the proximity of the silver."

"Great. I'm even more of a weirdo now."

Truthfully, I knew this day would come. The garlic thing had been getting worse. These days, I couldn't even go down the produce aisles without feeling shaky and weak. The other day, at Trader Joe's, I'd even blacked out a little. I'd been keeping my reaction to the bulbous root on the down-low. I was freaky enough as it was.

"Please, put it away."

He did so, tucking inside his shirt and sitting back. Immediately, I felt a wave of relief. "Don't worry, Sam. It won't get much worse than it is now. The garlic merely acts as a deterrent, a buffer, if you will. More than anything, it levels the playing field."

"You could kill me now, and I couldn't defend myself."

"Oh, you could. Like I said, it levels the playing field, not destroys it."

"Until you whip out the silver," I said, nodding toward both hips and his right underarm, all of which I could feel the silver radiating from, coming at me in short, hot bursts.

"Ah, you can feel the silver, too?"

I nodded, suddenly realizing just how vulnerable I was.

"A handgun under my arm, and two daggers at my side. There's a crossbow and silver-tipped bolts in the rental car."

"And you're giving me this rundown, why?"

"Because I don't trust vampires."

"Not even me?"

He stared at me long and hard, and his eyes, I realized were bluer than I remembered. Or maybe they were icier. Or deader. "No," he said.

"I have no intention of hurting you," I said.

"Nor do I."

"Then can we ditch the scary talk?" I asked. "You might deal with some real shitheads, but I'm not one of them. I fight this thing in me every day, and, so far, I'm winning."

"Until you don't."

"I don't intend for that to happen, Rand. Ever."

"Forever is a long time, Sam."

"It's my fight and no one else's."

"I know, Sam."

"You know what?"

"I know who is inside you, and I know why she is inside you, too."

"You get around."

He shrugged. "Some vampires try to talk their way out of the inevitable. I listen."

I nodded. "Then you—or your family—would be stupid to do something to let her out again."

"I couldn't agree more."

"Besides, we are past all of that, right?"

"You helped me find my kidnapped daughter," he said. "And for that, I will be eternally grateful."

"Am I still on your no-kill list?"

"You, and others you know."

"Then you will be excited to hear that you're on my no-kill list, too."

He grinned at that. I knew Rand now led the Brotherhood of the Blade, a group of elite assassins who made a habit of targeting the worst of the worst. His team was well-trained, well-armed, and ready for just about any situation. I suspected he had a team member nearby, keeping a lookout, which was customary. No members traveled alone, if they could help it, not even their fearless leader. Rand was a man who had launched a silver-tipped bolt into my shoulder and basically wrecked my night. In return? He got a free trip to Hawaii. Hardly even fair. Maybe he owed me one. Or two or three, since I also helped test their castle's security and tracked down his brother's killer. Is it possible that I'm too nice?

One didn't just become an elite vampire hunter, overseeing a crackerjack team stationed in Switzerland. Rand's journey had been long and torturous, a journey I wouldn't wish upon my worst enemy. Of course, a half a decade ago, I had thought Rand *was* my worst enemy. But as damaged as he was, as hurting as he was, he had accepted me for who I was. Good for me, literally. Maybe even good for him, too. Turns out, I can kinda hold my own in a fight, garlic be damned.

"I've been hearing stories about you, Sam."

"That I'm a great mother? That I can still make a helluva garlic-free spaghetti sauce, or so I'm told. Tastes like tangy mush to me, though."

He laughed. "Are you quite done, Sam?"

"My list goes on."

"I'm sure it does. Is the devil's destroyer on your list of accomplishments?"

I ducked at the question, glanced around. That the world was now absent its devil was something few realized. That people still believed in him was troubling. With belief, a dark one would step forward again and fulfill the role. At least, that's what I was told. For now, though, the world was devil-less, and, yeah, I supposed I knew the reason why. Okay, I *was* the reason why. I had personally killed the devil with a sword called, fittingly, The Devil Killer. Matter of fact, I still had it. Matter of fact, it was on my person now, hidden in a secret compartment that was technically a mini-parallel world. Why did I have it? Technically, I was still on the job as the Angel of Death's right-hand woman. Yes, the devil may be dead, but his many demons— created by him—were still on the loose. Call it mop-up duty. That said, the sword helped vanquish them. My new wings—presently in the form of black tattoos on my back—evened the playing field.

I'll say it again. I have to say it. Such words keep me grounded...

*My life is weird.*

I told Rand that he'd heard correctly, and gave him as much of a rundown as I felt he needed to know. And when I finished, there might have been some awe on his face. I'll admit, I liked seeing awe on his face. He bowed slightly and said, "Regarding the demons, I would like to formally offer you the services of the Brotherhood of the Blade."

I was grateful for the offer, but I said, "Demons are hard to kill."

"Perhaps, but we can aid you in other ways. We can hunt them, track them, report back on them. The world would be a far better place without these bastards."

Of that, I had no doubt. Since my battle with the devil three months ago, I hadn't heard again from Archangel Azrael, nor had I battled any actual demons, both of which were probably good things. I had a meeting tomorrow with Anthony's principal, and I didn't need to go in there fresh off a demon kill. (Anthony had "accidentally" driven the school's bully's head into a locker door.) Besides, I wasn't sure what my parameters were just yet. Meaning, did I just kill any ol' demon I spotted? Or did I wait for an official hit list from the Angel of Death? I suspected I would be used as needed, and when needed. One thing I knew: the demons were free radicals now, meaning, their leader and creator was gone. They were left to their own devices, and the devil had created many, many of them.

Hundreds, from what I understood. Did they all have to die? I mean, were they all terrible? Did any of them have any redeeming qualities? I didn't know, but the ones I had seen made the Dementors in Harry Potter look like Casper the Friendly Ghost.

"Thank you, Rand, but I'm sure you are busy with your own agenda."

He nodded and reached inside his jacket. I held my breath, although that wasn't saying much since I didn't officially need to breathe. When a well-armed vampire hunter reaches inside his jacket, vampires *should* hold their breath and prepare themselves for anything. I exhaled when he pulled out a small note.

"You okay, Sam?" He gave me a sly grin. Truce or not, I thought the man in front of me had a real hate for vampires—and, for good reason—and it was all he could do to uphold his end of the bargain. That he put a scare into one just now was, well, amusing to him.

"I think my heart might have stopped."

"How can you tell?"

"It's a saying, and you would do well to remember that I'm one of the good ones."

"I know, Sam. I admire and respect you."

"But sometimes you don't?"

"Sometimes, you scare me, too."

"I scare you?" I asked.

"Of course, Sam."

"I'm five-three and cowering at your necklace

of garlic."

"It's not your height, Sam. It's that you are even cowering at the garlic at all. It just shows how far you've descended."

"Ouch."

"I'm sorry, Sam. But it is obvious you are different from even the last time I saw you, a few years ago."

"Different how?"

"It's your eyes. They are not... human. No, they are far from human. The fire dances there almost permanently now, easy enough to see in this darkened room. Worse, you are forgetting to blink more and more. When last we met in L.A., you blinked often. You blinked almost normally. Now, not so much."

"Well, you know what I am, so why bother?"

"Exactly. Your disregard to maintain normalcy is... intimidating."

"You are intimidated?"

"Yes."

Okay, for some reason, that sent a thrill through me. Geez. Maybe I had descended further than I thought. I motioned to the paper. "Can we just get back to the list?"

"Right."

As he pushed it in my direction, I spotted the various names on it.

"It's a hit list," I said.

"Yes, Sam."

"Vampires?"

"And werewolves. One Lichtenstein creation. And one merman."

"Merman?"

"Him, in particular. We have evidence of his misdeeds for many, many decades. Over a century, in fact. He's a ruthless killer, and needs to be stopped."

"You plan to track him in the ocean?"

"Many of the mers are land-based, Sam. Like many of the weres, they can shift at will. There is evidence of him hanging out in Huntington Beach."

"The kayakers..."

"Likely victims."

I blinked. Mermaids and mermen were popping up now in my experience. Great. And, one of them, Kingsley had actually been married to in the last century. *Married.*

"And you plan on killing this merman?"

He held my gaze. "Yes, Sam."

"Does the garlic work on him, as well?"

"We do not know that, not yet. We'll see. We've only recently added other creatures to our kill list."

"Lucky for them."

"Very far from lucky, Sam."

"Do you enjoy killing?" I asked.

"I enjoy keeping people safe."

I knew he was lying, of course. The instant I had asked the question, a darkness rose up in his aura—

Rand was human, after all, and his aura was obvious to me. The darkness was... interesting. I suspected all the killings had attracted a low-level entity—not a dark master—perhaps your everyday serial killer. It appeared and hovered near the surface, then slinked away to be reabsorbed in the otherwise bright green and red aura.

"You can see him, can't you, Sam?"

Of course, I knew what he was talking about, and he knew what I was looking at. "Yes."

"It's a man, I think. I can feel him sometimes, hear him other times. He takes great delight in my killings."

"I see."

"It's not possession, Sam. It's attraction. He just hangs around, or so I believe."

It reappeared now, poking through the swirling staticky light surrounding his body. It dipped down below the roiling, ethereal colors. Such deep dives meant more than just a passing attraction. This thing was worming its way into him. How deep and how much influence it had on Rand, I didn't know. But it was there, and it was something to watch out for.

"How bad is it, Sam?"

"He's deeper than you think."

He nodded. "I will deal with him, whoever he is. For now, I have bigger fish to fry."

"A merman pun?"

"No, but it is now."

I grinned. "And why are you showing me this

list?"

"Simple, Sam. I respect you, and I respect your friends, too. You are doing good work out here, amazing work, unheard-of work."

"You're referring to my killing the devil and hunting his demons. Not my time following cheating husbands."

He smiled. "The former. I don't want to detract from that."

"By inadvertently killing one of my friends?"

"In a word: yes. Know anyone on the list?"

I took it and scanned it. There were nine names on the list. Two with "W" next to them, and one each with "M" and "L" next to them. I instinctively understood the letters to mean werewolf, merfolk and Lichtenstein monster. The name corresponding with the "M" was Barnaby. It was a name I didn't know. Neither did I know the others. I pushed the list back.

"Kill to your heart's content."

His was a dark grin, with just the corners of the lips moving, if that. And somewhere, deep, deep, deep inside his pupil, I might have seen a flash of light. His love for killing had opened him up to other dark forces that loved killing, too. I didn't need to read his mind to see it. There was going to be blood spilled—and soon—and it was going to be immortal blood. He might have been born into the hunter's bloodline, but this crazy son-of-a-bitch killed for the thrill of it, too.

"Now that we have that out of the way," I said, "I want to talk about my sire."

"What do you want to know, Sam?"

"I want to know why you gave his medallion to me."

# 21.

He didn't ask for clarification. He didn't ask me to repeat myself. Rand knew what I was talking about, and he leveled his considerable gaze at me. "Easy, Sam. He asked me to."

Like an allergic reaction, my tongue suddenly seemed too big for my mouth. But it wasn't allergies, since I hadn't had a sniffle in over a decade. When I finally found my voice, I asked, "What else did he say?"

"You're emotional, Sam."

"Do you care to share?"

Truth was, I wasn't sure how I felt about Rand in this moment. That he had extinguished the light of an amazing man, I had no doubt. But I also knew that Rand was just doing his job, fulfilling a role he'd been compelled to do for some time. And not just him... his bloodline. No reason to add this extra burden on the man, not that I cared too much if Rand carried such burdens. It just seemed... unnecessary, and a part of my life I didn't feel inclined to share with a man who had killed my one-father, even if he hadn't known J.C. was my one-time father. Then again, had he known, I doubted he would have cared, since, at the time, I had been his next target anyway. Just too much to process, and Rand wasn't the man I wanted to process it with.

Despite my reservations, he was right. I was emotional, and there was no holding it back. Not now. Not anymore. "I can't do this," I said.

"Do what?"

"Be civil," I said.

"I don't under—"

"You killed him, you motherfucker."

He blinked, sat back, and made an unconscious movement toward his jacket, stopping just short of reaching inside, which was a damned good idea, probably for both of us.

"You killed a great man and a loving father, a man who doggedly pursued the worst piece of shit on this planet. You killed him because it was in your fucking blood. You killed him because, yes, I can see you enjoy killing, no matter how much you claim it's your heritage. You're a cold-hearted, reckless, murderous piece of shit."

"Sam, calm down."

"The only thing keeping me from killing you

now is the very man whose life you extinguished. He was a good man who hurt no one, ever. Who lived to avenge my death."

"I know that now, Sam. Please, you're making a scene."

His hand was in his jacket, where the revolver was. Truth was, I wanted to kill him. I wanted to rip his throat out. Yes, I was weakened by the damn garlic and a proximity to silver, but fuck all that. I would fight through it, and I would fight him, too. No matter that he was nearly as fast as me, no way was he as strong, and no way could he stop me. No way, just no way...

I felt the tears streaming. The injustice of it all was just too much. I made to stand, but a hand lashed out and grabbed my wrist; it was Rand.

"Please, Sam. Don't leave."

I nearly ripped my hand away, but I sensed his strength. Wow, was he strong. But it was the look in his eyes that got me to finally, finally take a deep breath. Then another.

"Please, Sam. Sit."

I did so, slowly, noting all eyes were on us. Hell, even the music had stopped. The manager, I noted was coming our way, until I gave him a quick suggestion that he had to pee, and badly. He crossed his legs and grabbed his pee-pee, and veered off toward the restrooms.

"You do that?" asked Rand.

"I did."

He nodded. "I hope he makes it."

"He will. He doesn't really have to pee."

Rand nearly smiled, but didn't. His eyes squinted, even as his strong grip adjusted to now hold the top of my hand. His warm fingers curled around my small palm. For the first time, the distant, dancing fire in his eyes was gone.

"Tell me, Sam. What did you mean... avenge your death?"

But I couldn't find the words. Doing so would risk another outburst; in the least, a torrent of tears.

Rand studied me, his dark eyes searching. The real Rand sought answers. "I don't understand, Sam."

"He was... my father in another lifetime."

"Another life...?"

"A long, long story. He was my father and I was murdered, and my killer is still out there, killing others like me."

"Vampires?"

"No, witches. I had been a witch in my past life."

"But, Sam... I had it on good authority that he was one of the oldest vampires, one of the originals—wait, he'd been looking for your killer all this time?"

"He had."

"Geez, Sam. I didn't know."

"But even if you had, you would have killed him anyway. And me."

Rand said nothing, but I saw the tears in his own eyes. We both knew my words were true.

"My revelation changes nothing, of course."

"But it does explain why I thought I was about to get my head ripped off," said Rand. "And the experience did change how I do, um, business. I research more. I follow up more. I weigh the pros and cons. I ask questions of my vampire friends."

I nodded. I knew one of his team members was also a vampire.

*Strange bedfellows, indeed.*

"Had I done my due diligence with your, um, father..."

"Just call him J.C.," I said.

"With J.C., yeah, I would have bypassed him in an instant. It was obvious he wasn't a threat."

"No."

"I'm sorry, Sam."

"I know you are now. But then..."

"No, I had misgivings even then, Sam. I studied the man for months, watching his every movement. He knew I was out there. I sensed him sensing me. I watched him feed from the local wildlife, and even then, he didn't kill the critters. He was no threat, and I knew it."

"And you killed him anyway."

"I... I didn't know any better, Sam. It's what we did. It was what my family did."

"A poor excuse to kill a good man."

"That's just the thing, Sam. I didn't see him as a

man. I saw him as a monster. There is something within me that just... hates the things I hunt."

"You hate me?"

"I try not to."

"But you do?"

He took in some air. "I try not to. Let's leave it at that."

We were quiet for a heartbeat or two. Any of the lingering stares we got soon turned away. I quickly scanned the surrounding minds and verified no one had overheard us. The dueling pianos had long since started dueling again.

"Are we good, Sam?"

"As good as we can be."

"You were asking about the medallion. Would you like to hear more?"

I nodded, looked away from his eyes. There was real warmth there, even if there was confusion. I was his natural prey. I knew that. I knew he fought it when he was around me, and he probably fought when he was around his vampire team member. The good news was... he'd learned his lesson, even if it meant a good man—my one-time father—had to die.

"Sam, my aim that night was off, just enough that... J.C. survived the shot."

"A crossbow bolt?" I asked.

He nodded, and now, it was his turn to look away. "It had just missed his heart, but it had done enough damage to render him... immobile."

"What does that mean exactly?"

"The bolt had pinned him to a wall."

"Where?"

"In his home."

"You killed him in his home?"

"Yes, Sam."

"Was he asleep?"

"As terrible as you think I am, or was, I would not attack a defenseless target."

"But you attacked me when I first opened my hotel room door."

"I attacked you in the evening, when you were at full power. I gave you every chance to defend yourself, and you did."

"You could have gone in for the kill," I said, recalling the bolt plowing into my shoulder and spinning me into the hotel bathroom. The pain had been unreal.

"Truth be known, Sam, I couldn't do it."

"Do what?"

"Kill you."

"You aimed for my heart."

"But I paused, certainly long enough for you to turn away."

"Why did you pause?"

"I..." Rand opened his mouth and closed it again. "It was your sire. Already, his death was affecting me. It had, quite frankly, haunted me. I couldn't shake it, not like the others."

I watched the handsome, grizzled, blond-haired

man work through his own emotions. I noted the scars on his arms and knuckles. The man had gone to war for the mortals of the earth, whether they appreciated it or not. At the moment, I appreciated it not.

"Mostly, Sam, I remembered how he spoke of you."

"How did he speak of me?"

"With love, Sam."

My throat constricted, but I managed to speak anyway. "What did he say?"

"He was mortally wounded. I believe the bolt pierced his lungs and even, perhaps, his trachea. Instead of grabbing for it and trying to pull himself free, he reached for a medallion hanging around his neck. I approached him cautiously, to say the least. Vampires, especially older vampires, have more than a few tricks up their sleeves. Some have even learned minor enchantments, as I knew J.C. had."

"He knew you were onto him," I said, highly aware that I sounded like Dick Tracy but not caring one iota.

"Vampires are rarely surprised by my presence. Some flee. Some stay and fight. Most know of me and my talents. Most know it will be a fair-enough fight."

"Fair enough?"

"I'm just a mortal with a crossbow, Sam. I won't kill them in their sleep, but I do need to protect myself."

"You are more than mortal."

"No, Sam. I can die from salmonella poisoning like any other human. I can just channel the best of us when needed."

I caught the "us" part but let it slide. A speaking error only, obviously. Instead, I said, "Fine. What happened with the medallion?"

Rand nodded, held eye contact with me. Say what you will about the hunter, he had compassion, even if he was never, ever, truly sorry for his kills.

"He pulled it over his head with some difficulty and held it out to me. I told him to drop it, figuring it was a charm of some sort. He said he would not drop it, that it was a special gift. I stood there, with the next bolt notched and ready for the kill shot, and the old man—clearly the oldest-looking vampire I'd ever hunted—stared back at me with determination in his eyes. I asked him what he wanted me to do with it and he said to give it to you."

"At the time, did you know about me?"

"Of course, Sam. I had my..."

"Hit list."

"Yes."

"How did I find my way onto your list?"

He shook his head. "I can't give away all my secrets, Sam."

"Fine," I said. "Back to the necklace. I assume you took it."

Rand drummed his fingers on the scarred table, cracked his neck like a pro, then looked back at me.

"Against my better judgment, I took it from him."

"I assume nothing terrible happened?"

"No, Sam."

"Did he say anything else?"

"He did. He told me to tell his daughter that he loved her more than she would ever know, and that he was sorry he failed her twice. He said he was never more lost than when she was taken from him, and never more centered than when he found her again, time after time. He said his greatest gift was her and he was so proud to be her father. Sam... I didn't know he had been talking about you. I looked for his daughter, but found no indication of her anywhere... and soon forgot about his message... until now."

I briefly covered my eyes and asked Rand what happened next. After accepting the medallion and hearing J.C.'s final request, he'd said goodbye to the old man, who had nodded once and closed his eyes, and Rand had promptly plunged a silver dagger deep into his heart.

"I didn't feel right about it, Sam," said Rand.

"But you did it anyway."

"I had to. I'm sorry. The compulsion, at that time, was undeniable."

"And now?"

"Now, I have some control over it. Enough to make my own decisions."

"Well, good for you."

"And good for you, too, Sam. Again, I'm

sorry."

"What do you know of the Red Rider?" I asked suddenly, wanting to get off the subject of my one-father's death.

"Nothing, Sam. I'm sorry."

"But he is immortal... surely, he's on your radar... or the radars of your ancestors."

Rand shook his head. "From what I understand, he is a magical being first and foremost. He is not possessed by a dark master."

Rand stood and came around to my side of the table. He placed a heavy hand on my shoulder and, inside of me, Elizabeth recoiled at his touch. How many of her dark masters had he and his ancestors displaced? I didn't know, but she would know. Dozens, perhaps. Maybe even hundreds. No wonder why she'd recoiled.

"I hope you find the bastard, Sam. If you need my help, you have my number. I will be in L.A. for the next few weeks or so."

"Hunting mermen."

"One merman. Let's just hope I find him."

He patted my shoulder again, and headed off toward the door, weaving between the dueling pianos. He'd left behind a crisp hundred-dollar bill, which I hadn't seen until now. I grabbed it, held it up, protesting that it was way too much.

But he was already gone.

## 22.

I'd just paid the bill—or, rather, Rand had just paid—when the Angel of Death appeared by my side. Like right there, stride for stride, all glowing eight feet of him. I gasped and jumped and might have trembled a little. Since others didn't appear to see him, I kept my cool as best as I could, especially since most of the restaurant already thought I was freak.

I pushed through the glass double doors and stepped out onto Harbor Boulevard and into downtown Fullerton. The Angel of Death didn't step through the double doors; he walked through the brick façade of the old building itself... and continued by my side down a crowded sidewalk.

"It's been a while, Samantha."

"It has."

"I'm sorry if I startled you."

Squinting, I glanced up at the massive entity that should have blocked out the sun angling down in the same direction, except, being mostly transparent, the sun shone straight through him. "A giant, invisible angel suddenly appearing by my side? Why would I be startled?"

"Oh, others can see me, Sam. Look around."

I did, scanning the faces around us. There, a homeless man looked up from his seat against a wall across the street. Now, he was standing, watching us closely, mouth open.

"Why him?" I asked.

"There's more, look."

I did. A woman in a passing bus pressed her face against the smoky glass, eyes wide, breath fogging before her. A man coming toward us stopped in his tracks and dropped his cell phone. I snatched it up before it hit the ground. I tucked it in his pants pocket and nearly gave him a prompt to forget what he had seen, when I felt a warm hand on my shoulder.

"Leave him, Sam."

"But..."

The hand on my shoulder guided me around the man staring at us, whose mouth also hung open. I didn't blame him.

"But... they saw you. Won't that freak them out?"

"Not as much as you think, Sam."

A man on a passing bike hit his brakes and nearly went over his handlebars. Feet planted on the ground, he stared, mouth also hanging open. I was noticing a trend.

"But why them?" I asked, watching a woman from across the street stop and stare, both hands clutching white gift bags. She nearly dropped them but managed to keep it together enough not to.

"Those who asked can see me."

"Asked to see the Angel of Death?"

"No, Sam. Asked to see a miracle. Asked to see proof that there is something beyond their five senses. Asked for something to believe in. First and foremost, Sam, I am an angel."

"An archangel," I said.

"Indeed, Sam. And, as such, I also work as an agent for something greater than me."

"God."

"God, the Creator, the Source, the All That Is, the Origin."

"The Big Tuna."

"If that works for you, Sam."

"Have you seen God?"

"We all have, Sam. Every day. Every second. Every atom is infused with the breath of God."

"Okay, that's the boring answer. How about giving me the answer I'm really looking for?"

"You are asking if I have seen the face of God?"

"His face, his hair, any part of him, really."

"God makes frequent appearances here on

earth... and in many other worlds of his creations, disguised as one of his creations. I use the masculine here for the sake of convenience. God is pure energy and without gender, of course."

"Of course."

I thought back to my conversation with God just a few months ago. It had taken place in my minivan, via a pen and pad of paper. True, I'd had similar such conversations; that is, through automatic writing. But this conversation had been... different. This conversation came with a trip to heaven, a trip that I'd been hesitant to speak about to anyone. I both wanted to forget what I had seen, and wanted to think about it continuously. But knowing I would never see this paradise again was too much to deal with, and so I didn't. I did my best to put it out of my thoughts. Interestingly, I also thought back to the man who had called himself Jack, a man I'd met at a Denny's nearly six years ago, a man who had known everything about me... and did not judge me.

"And love?" I asked. "God is also love?"

"Love is a vague concept, Sam, that many people—many humans, at least—get wrong. I would suggest that God is... benevolent energy. Yes, that works. Benevolence for his creations goes without saying."

"Of course," I said. "Although it doesn't hurt, you know, to actually say it."

The angel, who somehow matched me stride for stride, although his strides were much, much larger than mine, looked down at me. His beautiful, golden hair sat unmoving on his broad shoulders, and, for all intents and purposes, Thor himself was walking with me down Harbor Boulevard, mostly ignored by those who couldn't see him—or who hadn't asked for a miracle.

"The love that flows from the Source Entity, Sam, is a continuous stream of unending joy and uplifting inspiration. It is life itself. It is the air we breathe, the thoughts we think, the passion we feel. When one learns how, one can tune into this flowing well-being at any time, all day long. Once done, miracles happen, inspiration happens, creation happens. Humans have a bad habit of doubting this love, shutting it off, and avoiding it all together. When that happens, well, you can see the results around you."

"God punishes?" I asked.

"God expands, Sam. God expands even when he's been cut off completely."

"You're saying God benefits even while others suffer?"

"Through their suffering, they ask for more, Sam. And through their asking, God expands to answer. It's a beautiful thing. All benefit."

"Even angels?"

"The entire Universe benefits from the expansion."

"Why?"

"With more creation, there are more options.

More tools to play with, more thoughts to think, more worlds to explore."

"But why must there be suffering?"

"There needn't be suffering, Sam. But there does need to be recognition of something wanted."

I nodded. "And if all was rosy and peachy-keen, there would be no reason for something wanted."

"Yes, Sam. It's why you came here. Why everyone came here."

"To a messed-up Earth?"

"To opportunity, Sam. It's all in how you look at it. It is the same with suffering. Why suffer, when blessings are right around the corner. Why wallow, when answers are at your fingertips? Have faith, foster positive expectations, and the world is yours. More humans than you know receive the blessings of heaven, although some sooner than others."

"What do you mean by blessings? Does God reward?"

"A good question, Sam. I said earlier, when humans ask, God expands. That means, God answers... the expansion means God becomes that which is asked for or yearned for or hoped for. It's waiting and ready."

"Ready for who?"

"Those who are ready."

"How does one get ready?"

"How does one receive any blessing, Sam? How does anyone, anywhere, receive that which they most want?"

"Does the answer have something to do with Oprah?"

"No, but she is an example of one who is tapped into the vibration of abundance."

"Vibration?"

"Everything has a vibration, Sam. You asked how does one get ready? The answer is simple: find a way to practice the feeling of the desire, the vibration of it, and watch it begin to unfold in your life. Generally, it will begin with ideas... with manifestations to follow. For every great business, great relationship, or, quite frankly, anything of worth and note in this world, began as a desire born from life experience. And from that experience, which, admittedly, could be painful, a yearning was launched. That yearning was heard by the Creator."

"And he what... created it?"

"In essence, yes. Created vibrationally. Expanded and acted upon, and is waiting for you, dear one, to summon it into existence."

"And if someone doesn't summon it?"

"It waits, calling to you sometimes, haunting you other times, beckoning, waiting, vibrating."

"Waiting for someone to get ready?"

"Yes, Sam."

"And what happens when someone *is* ready?"

"The thing desired—whatever it might be—begins flooding to you. First with ideas, then with smaller manifestations, until it fully manifests."

"And then what?" I asked.

"Enjoy it, revel in it... and get ready for the next manifestation. It never ends, Sam. Every day, all day long, you are asking and yearning and hoping, and God is listening and expanding and holding your desire for you. You need only to..."

"Get ready for it."

"Exactly."

"Who wouldn't receive the blessings?"

"Those who doubt, Sam. Those who hate. Those who focus more on the not having of something, than the having of it. Those who speak of ill instead of health. Those who speak of lack instead of abundance."

"And what if someone had never been taught such concepts? What if someone only knows pain and suffering?"

"Such concepts are not hard to understand, Sam. There is enough literature to show the way, from the Bible to other holy books, from inspired leaders and coaches, from enlightened friends who might say just the right thing at just the right time. The truth is, Sam, we all learn from watching others. It is not very hard to hear a successful woman talk and note she speaks of only the good in her life. It is not hard to hear the blessed holy man speak of love and good health only. It is not a challenge to note that the healthy among you speak only of health. Such clues go far."

"And if someone still doesn't pick up on such clues?" I asked.

"Oh, they will. One way or another. That is one of the purposes of the guardian angel. To show the way to better-feeling choices, to happier-leaning thoughts."

We turned a corner, and I headed for the parking lot where the momvan was located. "I never asked to be a vampire," I said. "I never asked to have heaven ripped out from under me. So explain that."

"I have limited access to what is in your heart, Sam. But with every manifestation in the world, there was a vibrational connection to it, even if it was unwanted. It benefits the human greatly to keep thoughts positive, eager, and hopeful. Basically, to stay as happy as possible, for as often as one can. Happiness is not so hard to find, is it? You are alive. You are free. You can explore this amazing world. Your imagination knows no bounds. Create and play, and bask in the joy of life, and you will see blessings rain down upon you."

"Um, I'm not sure that answered my question."

"It did, Sam. On some level, you wanted more. On some level, you wanted to be empowered. On some level, you asked to see the magic in the world."

In that moment, an older lady pushing a wire basket, looked up, gasped, and held her heart. Azrael smiled down at her, and tears sprang from her eyes. We moved past her.

"Just like these people have asked to see a miracle."

"Yes, Sam."

"But a vampire? C'mon. I never asked for *that*."

"No, Sam. But you asked for the essence of it. You wanted to be a hero at work. You wanted to be a hero for those in need. A hero for your children. Think back, Sam."

*A heroine.* I nodded, nearing the parking lot. That I was being followed by a hulking, beautiful, blond-haired Angel of Death probably should have excited me more than it did. But it didn't, not now. Now, I wanted answers.

I shrugged. "I wanted to see miracles, too. I mean, it wasn't something I ran around saying to everyone, but I was always interested in the world behind the veil, so to speak. As a kid, I always tried to fly. I was always jealous of the birds of the air. I thought for sure, if I just willed it enough, I would fly."

"And now you have wings."

"All kids want to fly," I said.

"Think, Sam. In how many dreams were you flying?"

"Many," I said. "Dozens. Hundreds, maybe."

"And in these dreams, did the flying feel natural?"

"Yes. But, and I can't emphasize this enough, they were just dreams."

"Dreams operate two-fold, Sam. One, they can remind you of what's active in your vibration. And two, they can be an indicator of what is to come."

"Still, I'm sure many people dream of flying."

"They do, Sam. And these people do so in their own way. In planes, in hang gliders, in parachutes, high-diving, bungee-jumping, and other creative ways humans have found to soar through the air. Yours might be one of the most creative."

"My wings?"

"Indeed."

"You're saying I attracted all of this... vampirism, blood-sucking, Elizabeth, Talos, wings, the Devil Sword..."

"Yes, Sam. All of it. Quite simply, becoming a vampire was the best way for you to allow all your dreams to come true."

"But heaven was stolen from me."

"Immortality was given to you. It is all in your perception, Sam."

"But there is so much more going on to why I became what I became. The dark masters, Ishmael's betrayal... some of this has been going on for centuries, many, many lifetimes."

"And so it has, Sam... and it's culminated in this one. It's called momentum. And to answer you your heart's greatest desire, the earth had to move mountains and shift realities to make it happen. But happen, it did."

"All for me?"

"All for everyone. All creations, everywhere, get the same attention from the Source Entity."

"But I am kinda special, though, aren't I?" I

said, winking, getting my car keys out.

"Yes, Sam. But so is everyone."

"You couldn't throw me a bone, could you?"

Azrael smiled and paused at the minivan. That my old hunk of junk could occupy the same space as this radiating, pulsating, hunk of angel magic was proof that God had a sense of humor.

"Fine," I said. "Have you seen God? And not just his physical incarnation here on Earth. And no boring shit—crap—like we see him every day, in everything. I mean, the real God."

"I know what you mean, Sam. The Creator dwells at the highest levels of vibration and the highest dimensions of thought."

"Well, good for him."

"Good for us all, Sam. If not for his desire to expand, we would not be here."

"So how does one reach the Origin?"

"For those outside the reincarnation loop—that is to say, immortals like you—they will meet him someday should they perish here on Earth."

"Where they will be reabsorbed or something."

"Yes, Sam."

"I don't want to be reabsorbed," I said. "I don't want to die. But I want to meet him. Or her. Or it."

"For the sake of simplicity, the masculine works fine."

"Yeah, yeah. Except I did meet him, though, didn't I?"

Azrael studied me, and as he did so, the hair on

his wide shoulders lifted and fell gently, as if he alone were hovering at the bottom of the ocean. Finally, he nodded. "The entity you met was not the Origin, nor could it be, for the Origin is..."

"Without body, yeah, yeah. I get it. Then who did I meet?"

"You met the incarnated version of the entity who plays the role of God."

"Say again?"

"You'll recall that the entity who was the devil came into being because he was, quite literally, summoned into existence. The version of God you met face-to-face is also such a being. One who has come forward to fulfill a role."

"The role of God?"

"Yes."

"That's quite a role."

"Yes, Sam."

"Have you met this God?"

"Indeed."

"He's God, but he isn't God?"

"In a way, yes."

"Is he a creator?"

"Yes."

"Is he a fake?"

"No."

"But he's not the Origin Entity?"

"Not by a long shot."

"But he can perform miracles?"

"He can create planets. Is that miracle enough?"

"Er, yes."

I paused, jangling my keys, both wondering why the Angel of Death even bothered to show up, and, conversely, trying to rescramble my beliefs. This was a lot to take in. "And what of other gods? You know, other religions, other belief systems?"

"If the belief is real and without doubt, the entity will manifest."

"So this planet is swarming with gods and devils?"

"And angels and demons and everything in between."

"Mind... blown. Again."

"The devil was just one such entity created to fulfill a role. And, as we speak, another is coming forward to answer the call."

"The call of the devil?"

"Yes."

"Then why bother killing him?"

"You tell me, Sam."

"He was after my family. My daughter, in particular."

"That is how I see it, too. You didn't *have* to kill him. You could have negotiated, you could have come to a truce. There were other options."

"He wanted to die," I said. "It was his exit point."

"There were many factors in play. It is what it is, as they say."

"Years ago, deep in meditation, I caught a

glimpse of the Origin." That had been on an island in the Pacific Northwest.

"And so you did."

"Why are you here?" I suddenly asked. "Now, in this parking lot?"

He paused.

"Let me guess..." I began.

"Yes, Sam. One such demon is nearby and is wreaking havoc in the life of a young artist. He has prayed for help. You can be the answer to his prayers."

"You're giving me my first assignment?"

"Indeed, Sam."

"Fine," I said. "First, I have more questions."

"Fire away."

And I did, and the beautiful creature did his best to answer them all, and when he was done, an address appeared in my thoughts. And just as it did, Azrael disappeared.

Poof, just like that.

## 23.

Okay, now I know what it must feel like when I disappear in front of others. My poor brain. It's stuff like this that seriously makes me question my sanity. One moment, a tall, beautiful angel, the next moment, gone.

*Yeah, yeah,* I thought. *Get over it. Disappearing people are the least of your worries.*

That said, having taken down the devil just months ago, I wasn't too terribly concerned about one little old demon. Then again, the demons I had fought in Kingsley's house had been nasty as hell... and as ferocious as can be.

I took in some silly air, let the silly air out, took in some more, then stepped into my car. I plugged the still-fresh address in my thoughts into the Garmin on my dashboard, nodded to myself encouragingly, then started the minivan and headed off to fight a demon.

*\*\**

*I'm a mom,* I thought, as I drove south along Harbor, in the opposite direction of where I lived. *Not a demon slayer.*

Then again, I wasn't previously a devil slayer, either, but now, here I am.

Personally, I adhered more toward the "live and let live" motto. But, if a young person's life was in imminent danger, well, I'd just take a look and see what the situation was. Then again, hadn't I signed up to be the Angel of Death's assassin for, like, ever? I thought I had. I think. I was so desperate to beat the devil, some of the details of my first meeting with Azrael were a bit sketchy.

"Yup," I said, drinking from my water bottle and thinking back. "I agreed to it. At least as long as those demons are around."

Of course, I didn't have to accept the Devil Killer sword. I could have bypassed it and, as the glorious creature had suggested, negotiated my way out of my conflict with the devil.

Yeah, right. The devil had his sights set on my daughter and her ability to read any creature's mind, mortal or immortal, angelic or demonic. Yeah, the devil had to go, and if I had to slay some demons in the process... so be it.

Live and let live... a good motto... until they came for your daughter.

Yeah, I'm a mom first... and a whole lot of other things second, third, and fourth. Might as well add demon slayer to the mix.

If not for my attack twelve years ago, I would be working a crap-ton of cases right now with Chad Helling at HUD. Undoubtedly, we would be out following up on witnesses or checking in on federal housing applicants or contacts. And if we were lucky, we might even find ourselves part of a bigger sting. If we were unlucky, we would show up to empty house after empty house. Then again, some of those moments were the best. The banter between partners was priceless.

I hadn't wanted to go demon hunting, at least not at this moment. I had wanted to see the Librarian, aka, the Alchemist, aka, Archibald Maximus, aka Max. I had a shit-ton of questions about my father... and about the Red Rider.

So many questions... but here I was, off on my first demon-hunting assignment.

I wanted to curse, but I didn't. Nope, because the address was coming up and my inner alarm was already pinging softly... and growing steadily louder. I pulled up in front of a small home in Anaheim, just a few miles from Disneyland. The home, with its broken windows and overgrown grass, beer bottles and cigarette butts everywhere, was clearly not the happiest place on earth.

I stepped out of my momvan, my adrenaline thumping in my ears, my heart actually picking up its pace.

The good news, the Devil Killer was always with me, hidden in a secret pouch that kinda existed in an alternate reality, if what I'd heard was correct.

The bad news was... I hadn't a clue what I was walking into.

## 24.

The young artist's home was... unique, to say the least.

As I approached the front steps, which led up to a wide front porch, I noted a cartoonish painting of the moon in a window next to the front door. More paintings littered the porch, some of which were broken in half or bent and twisted, like a perfectionist artist was just not happy with his work. I looked at one of the folded paintings... and was impressed. Clearly an original, it depicted a snow-capped mountain, clouds and surrounding forest. Sure, maybe it was a bit simple, but the painting had real pop, and I almost recognized the mountain. Mount Shasta, perhaps? Maybe.

I heard a bang from inside, then a shout. Then another, louder bang.

Gunshots? Fireworks? I hadn't a clue.

I eased up the wide porch and puzzled over the array of many discarded and damaged paintings—each more beautiful than the next, and all of majestic landscapes—and moved toward the front door. I was about to knock but decided against it. My inner alarm had reached its saturation point, and backed off a little, which meant danger was still high, but it also didn't want to overwhelm my senses... in particular, my hearing. My inner alarm is cool like that.

These days, I don't carry a gun. Back in the day, yes. Back in the day, I might have had Chad go around back while I covered the front, each with our guns drawn. Then again, back in the day, I wouldn't have been given the assignment of removing a demon.

*Let's get real, Sam,* I thought, reaching down into that invisible pocket near my waist. *You're not here to remove it. You're here to destroy it.*

True enough.

My groping hand... now feeling oddly cool as it briefly disappeared from view... found the hilt of the sword. I proceeded to pull it free from its invisible, otherworldly sheath. And the sword kept coming and coming, until finally, in all its obsidian brilliance, it flashed dully in my hands, easily three feet long. Had I been mortal, it might have been heavy. Now... well, now it felt just about perfect in my hand. I resisted the urge to toss it from palm to palm. I wasn't *that* cocky. There was a real demon here, after all, and if the Angel of Death was to be believed—and my own continuous inner alarm—there was real danger here.

I paused briefly, gathered myself, and did what any demon hunter would do...

I kicked the door open.

\*\*\*

I saw more paintings, everywhere.

But these were not so lovely, and certainly not so idyllic. These were, and this could be open to interpretation, pictures of hell itself. Not that I would know. But if hell was anywhere close to what I was seeing now, it was surely a terrifying place.

*Hells,* I corrected, knowing everyone had their own private hell, literally.

The paintings were everywhere, on walls, lined up in rows, thrown over the carpet and furniture. The macabre paintings even covered other paintings, as hellfire and torment overlapped with crashing waves, beaches. In nearly all the paintings, dark, clawed figures huddled around burning humans, chained humans, or dissected humans. Other creatures clamored around the paintings, red-eyed creatures that clung to walls that were not unlike the creatures I'd seen at my one-time father's mansion.

*Not his mansion anymore,* I reminded myself.

*Your mansion now.*

Okay, that was a thought for another time. Truth was, I still couldn't wrap my head around the idea that I was now the proud owner of a very large home in the hills of Fullerton. And I certainly wasn't going to try and wrap it around it now, not with more banging coming from the back of the house.

I held out the sword before me like I knew what I was doing with it. Well, I kinda did. I'd gotten a crash course in sword fighting by the Archangel Michael himself—the warrior angel, mind you—just a few months ago. But it wasn't like I went around practicing with the thing. Then again, as I crept through the smallish house, past painting after gruesome painting—(the one next to me featured a severed, screaming head)—I kinda, sorta wished I knew what the hell I was doing. The sword, I knew, had to be driven through the heart of these things, just as it had gone through the heart of the devil himself.

Something crashed loudly and the whole house shook. There, down the hall and through a doorway, I saw a figure—a human figure—flash by... and *bang*. He slammed into the wall, although he had briefly disappeared from my line of sight. Yes, that was the sound I'd heard. The man—I was sure it was a man—was hurling himself into a wall. Or being hurled into it. I didn't know yet.

Red paint—looking for all the world like

blood—dripped down the hallway walls. And yeah, dammit, my stomach growled, and I hated myself all the more for it. Who the hell gets hungry at a time like this?

A vampire roaming around in the light of day, with her two magical rings on, that's who.

I ignored the bloody paint. I also ignored the filthy clothes... and what I assumed were piles of human waste. Sadly, I couldn't ignore the stench of urine and filth and vomit splatters. I gagged, but held it down. Somehow, I even ignored what I was sure was a patch of human scalp with human hair. I ignored it all, and eased down the hallway, sword in hand...

## 25.

The figure flashed before me again, this time crossing the hallway and going from one room into another.

He was a youngish man, maybe in his late twenties. Long shaggy hair, shirtless, skinny, pale, almost vampiric. Unmistakable was the blood pouring down from his body. I suspected a head wound. In fact, I suspected he had been hammering his head into the wall, which was the banging I'd heard.

Sweet mama.

The smell of blood filled the air, and the coppery sweetness of it was intoxicating, to say the least. My body was a combination of factors. Most of my talents and skills came from the wholeness of my soul, contained in this little five-foot, three-inch frame. Some of my weaknesses and cravings and, quite frankly, the magic that animated what should have been a corpse, came from Elizabeth. That magic craved blood... unlike any craving I've ever had before. I suspected blood kept this body alive... or, rather, kept the magic active. Should I someday die... Elizabeth would return to the Void where she would await yet another human host... and another. All while I got reabsorbed into the Creator, like something out of a horror movie, except with a lot more light and love. Or so I'm told.

I ignored the blood as best as I could. And how long had it been since I fed last? Days, I think. Shit, I probably should have had a nip last night. On a personal level, I found it revolting. Then again, what other levels were there?

I'd gotten good at denying myself—and denying Elizabeth. So, as challenging as it was, I pushed aside the thoughts of feasting on blood, and pushed Elizabeth down the rabbit hole of my mind, too, and eased down the hall. She wanted blood, but she also wanted me to get the hell out of here. She was no idiot. She could hear my warning bells going off as easily as I could. She didn't want her precious host hurt. She didn't want me hurt, since I was the bridge, somehow, between worlds.

*But wasn't this part of your master plan? To destroy the devil and his demons? Oh, you were only interested in destroying the devil? The demons you were okay with? Well, it was kind of a package deal, and I'm in this for life. So, yeah.*

## VAMPIRE SIRE

A growl vibrated the very floors from the room on the right.

Mama, that sounded terrifying.

Last time I'd fought a demon, it—or they—had come for my daughter. Indeed, it had been an all-out attack on Kingsley's mansion, which he was still cleaning up after. He'd lost a few friends that night, Lichtenstein monsters all, and it was a sore spot that I mostly avoided talking about with him. It had been tough hearing him howl in agony that night, and his sour moods lately were, undoubtedly, a result of his losses. That said, four such monsters still lived with him in his mansion, of which Franklin was one. I considered all of them friends, scars and all. Even that cantankerous head butler.

So, yeah, the last I'd seen one of these things— demon, that is—I'd been literally thrown into action with no time to think.

Now, I was the fool for walking in on one. Keeping my end of this demon-killing bargain suddenly seemed like a very bad idea.

At the door to the bedroom in question, I was about to say something to the young man inside when my warning bells rang so sharply and loudly that they literally drove me back the way I'd come, stumbling back through the hallway, just as the wall adjacent to where I had been standing exploded out.

Now standing before me was one hell of a big demon.

\*\*\*

It looked like all the others I'd battled, only bigger. Then again, it was also crowded into a narrow human-sized hallway, which it filled completely.

Truth was, it looked kind of badass. Hulking, angular, hooded, with red eyes. What was up with these red eyes, anyway? I was pretty sure it would be anyone's worst nightmare. That I couldn't see its face was probably a good thing. Yes, I might be the Angel of Death's right-hand woman, but I still get the crap scared out of me, and now was no different. Maybe more so. Just about everything leaves the mind when confronted with such a thing. My instinct was to run, and run, I did.

Sort of. Rather, I backpedaled through the hallway, dragging the sword over the wooden floor. Its razor-sharp tip left behind long, smoking grooves. Oopsie.

Speaking of smoking, lots of the stuff was rising up from the hood, swirling and filling the hallway. It watched me briefly before lurching forward, its shoulders comically hunched, clearly too big for the space. The demon didn't seem to mind the drywall particle dust that coated its black robe.

And why a demon needed a robe—that was my last coherent thought before the thing charged me.

I raised the Devil Killer before me...

\*\*\*

This demon was faster than I remembered any of the ones I'd fought being.

Then again, it was clearly bigger too. Maybe a new class of demon? Either way, a lightning-fast swipe of its whooshing claws launched me off my feet and sent me flying through the air to the middle of the living room floor, where I landed on my shoulder with a bone-crunching snap. The snap part was critical. I knew immediately I'd broken my collarbone.

With the thing crashing down the hallway toward me, I sat up. *Ouchie.* Yes, I'd definitely broken my collarbone. My right collarbone, no less.

The bastard.

It roared into the living room, pulverizing the corner of the hallway wall as it did so. Okay, I might be in trouble. My right arm was, after all, my sword-fighting arm.

I found my feet faster than any person should. One moment, I was on my back, and the next, I was on my feet in the *en garde* position.

Like a scene out of *The Princess Bride*, I tossed the Devil Killer into my left hand... and immediately lunged to the side as another clawed hand slashed down from above with a shrill whistle, clearly intending to slice me into quarters. I felt the whoosh of hot air.

Sweet mama. So much for the myth that demons

were only energy beings.

I knew they weren't, of course. They were definitely solid matter. I had seen their destruction to Kingsley's mansion. I would also learn just today (thanks to my talk with Azrael) that such demons can only hold this physical form for so long. And they did so at their own peril, meaning, this was when they were most vulnerable... and most ferocious.

*Then why do they materialize at all?* I had asked just a half hour earlier.

*It is their instinct to fight, Sam. It was how they were created.*

*Why not just flee?*

*See my prior answer.*

*But why fight me at all? For all they know, I'm just there to sell them Avon.*

*They know who you are, Samantha Moon. They sense the Devil Killer on you.*

*Then why not avoid me altogether?*

*Like angels, they exist in a hive mind. What one knows, they all know. They are willing to sacrifice themselves for the greater good, although there is nothing good about them.*

*Do they have souls? Where do they go when killed?*

*They are reabsorbed, Sam. As far as souls... I cannot answer that in a way that would be satisfactory to you.*

*Do you have a soul, Azrael?*

*See my prior answer.*

*Can you try to answer? Please, this will help me understand what I am up against.*

*Demons were created by the devil.*

*But the Bible says...*

*That one third of the demons fell with the devil from heaven and turned evil, right alongside him. You know otherwise, Sam.*

*Yes.*

*The devil, among his many attributes, was a Creator in his own right. He chose to create foot soldiers... and he chose to create the many hells.*

*Which still exist?*

*Yes, Sam. They have not gone anywhere.*

*Because it's up to the occupant to decide when they've had enough... and to go to the light?*

*Exactly. Hell is merely an illusion, albeit a painful one. Or as painful as each occupant will allow.*

*Okay, fine... what are demons, then?*

*They are fragments of the devil himself, Sam. As a creator, he infuses each of his creations with something of himself.*

*But no soul?*

*No, Sam. Only entities created from the Origin have what you would call souls.*

*Are you created from the Origin?*

*No, Sam. Not directly. I was created by another such creator.*

*The entity known as God,* I had said.

*Yes, Sam.*

*And should you die, you would get reabsorbed into him?*

*No, Sam. Like you, my fate is similar.*

*You would go home to the Origin?*

*Yes. All life, ultimately comes from the Origin. Those without souls, or those with no heavenly anchor, return to him.*

*And even though the devil is dead, his creations live on?*

*Apparently so.*

*You did not know?*

*This was, admittedly, a first for me.*

*Killing the devil?*

*Yes, Sam.*

*So we're in uncharted territory here?*

*Kind of.*

*Why does it make me nervous hearing an archangel say 'kind of'?*

*Because you want your world explainable in rational terms.*

*And sometimes, it's not.*

*More accurately stated: sometimes, the question has never been posed before; therefore, the answer is not known. I would suggest this is such a case. But, to wit, the demons do live on. So, by default, we already have your answer.*

*And why must we remove them?*

*The demons were created by the devil for one purpose only, Sam. To wreak havoc. In essence, they do not have free will. They are, quite frankly, proxies of the devil himself. Extensions, if you will.*

*But doesn't everything have a right to live, and all that? Even demons?*

*Does the mosquito have a right to live? Does the flea have a right to live? Does the tick burrowing in your skin have a right to live? Does the worm infesting your intestines have a right to live? Why not just let them feed? Why remove them at all?*

*Who's to say who lives or dies?*

*It is the dance of life, Sam. Creatures who invade, harass, cause harm to others, risk being removed by the inflicted.*

*And who's to decide who's causing harm or not?*

*We all get to decide.*

*And, by default, we decide who lives or dies?*

*The short answer is yes. Humans make such decisions every day. They execute killers, they trap vermin, they hunt for meat.*

*And some kill for pleasure.*

*Fewer than you think, Sam.*

*And who decided to kill all the demons? I know I didn't make that decision.*

*No, Sam. But you are an agent of those who made such decisions.*

*And who would that be? The angels?*

*In a way, yes. But the real answer is... humanity at large. A general consensus, among those who believe, is that demons are not worthy of existence, that demons have run afoul of the general desire of peace and love.*

*Peace and love is the general desire?*

*The majority's desire, yes.*

*Then why not extend the love to the demons?*

*Why not extend the love to the mosquito feasting on your arm? Why does the human swat it into oblivion? Why not lovingly allow it to drink?*

I shrugged. *People don't want to be a food source, especially for insects. People don't want to deal with the resulting bump that might itch for days, too. And people don't want to be exposed to possible diseases.*

*The desire of the insect is usurped by the desire of the human; the insect, if spotted in time, is destroyed.*

*But sometimes, the insect wins.*

*Often, the insect wins. Just as, too often, the demon in its many forms, wins, too. But not anymore, Sam.*

*Because the majority's desire is to rid the earth of demons?*

*Yes.*

*And how do you know the Earth's majority desire?*

*I don't, but my Creator does.*

*God?*

*Yes.*

*The man I met, so many years ago?*

*Was an incarnation of God, but yes. That was*

*he.*
*And God hears the call of all?*
*No, Sam. Just those who believe.*
*And he sent the angels to kill them?*
*No, Sam. He sent you.*

\*\*\*

This thing was real, it was three-dimensional, and it wanted to straight-up kill me.

Whether or not it could, I didn't know. I might be immortal, but being severed in quarters would probably do the trick. Its claws were seriously no joke. Azrael had told me earlier that demons can briefly possess the physical form. And it is in such a form that they are easiest to kill. It is in such a form, that they, in turn, can kill, too. I had to strike quickly before said demon blew its wad, so to speak, and was forced to retreat in a black mist to fight another day.

The demon, I knew, could possess, well, anything. From humans to houses, to books to mannequins. What it had been doing here in this house, I hadn't a clue, but judging by the bloody nature of the recent paintings, I would suggest it had been possessing the crap out of the young artist himself.

No, it wasn't in my nature to wantonly kill. But it was in my nature to help those who needed it, even if they didn't know they needed it, or didn't ask. Hell, if anything, I was breaking and entering.

Now, however, I was defending myself. And yeah, I kinda had to agree: the world would probably be a lot better off without this... thing... haunting it and wreaking its havoc. So here I was, a demon hunter, armed with the Devil Killer... and now sporting a broken collarbone that, even now, I sensed was stitching itself up. But it would need more than a few seconds. It would need a full day or two.

Although I wasn't into killing for killing's sake, I was into saving my hide, and ridding the artist of the very thing charging me now...

I dove to the side—and promptly broke my collarbone all over again.

That said, the four sharp, black, curved claws that slashed the air just above me would have done a hell of a lot more damage. From my back, I parried the next slash and the next, each raining down on me faster and harder than the swipe before. Claws clashed against obsidian and metal in an explosion of light and sulfur.

Its next swing was less of a swing and more of a power drive; as in, it was meant to drive me down through the floorboards. But I saw the demonic hand coming down in time to turn my sword, tip up...

...and watched the point sink deep into the dark palm, itself surprisingly human-like in appearance, although easily three or four times the size of my own. The claws—or talons—clacked as black blood poured down the blade and flooded over my hand.

Some of the ceiling broke free as the demon reared its head back and screamed bloody murder. It pulled its hand free and lurched back, even as more of the black stuff sprayed me from the opening. I screamed, too, as the shit burned... and was just oh-so gross. I had just wiped my eyes free of the bloody poison, certain that I had gone momentarily blind in the process, when I took note of a considerably diminished demon. Now, it just rose right up to the ceiling, perhaps ten feet tall in all. And pissed as hell. The thing was, I knew, using up whatever fight it had left in it. Now was the time to attack. And attack, I did.

Having the thing slightly more diminutive wasn't an advantage for me, although it might have saved the small house from further destruction. Truth was, it could move more freely, slashing at me faster than I remembered these things ever moving. Everything about this demon was different. It was bigger, badder, nastier.

It swung a clawed hand, then another and another, and I awkwardly fended off each blow, trusting my speed more than anything. I might be faster and stronger than ever, but I was still clumsy as hell with my left hand. And... well, that, and it was still late afternoon. The sun hadn't yet set, and that was a damn shame because I really kick ass after sunset.

Its next swipe came at me sideways, its arm

unnaturally long, made even longer by the claws. Unlike the movies, sadly, I wasn't gifted with acrobatic abilities. Teleporting, yes. Mind reading, yes. Backward, graceful flips, not so much.

In this case, I parried the claws and leaped over the arm, but my heel got caught in what was the demonic equivalent of a thumb. The claw both slashed my New Balance shoes, and sent me spinning in the air. I landed on... yes, my broken collarbone, and tears sprang from my eyes. With my inner warning blaring loudly, I rolled to my left, screaming, just as four claws drove deep into the hardwood floor next to me.

The demon, now noticeably shrinking, yanked at claws that had been seemingly fused with the wood itself. The sword had gone skittering off, and like Thor, minus the pecs, I held open my hand for it and envisioned its swift return to me. It came *slinging* back with a metallic twang, and I caught it neatly, spun it, and promptly drove it into the demon's exposed back, roughly where its heart would be, which I doubted it had, but whatever. It threw its shoulders back, screamed bloody murder, and crumpled to the floor, black blood spilled out like an oil slick. Seconds later, the blood... and body... began steaming and hissing. Moments later, there was nothing left but a demon-shaped stain on the hardwood floor... but even that began to fade too.

What happened next to the demon, I neither

knew nor cared. I think Azrael himself might escort the demon back to the Origin, although not all the way back, since Azrael himself had claimed never to have seen the Big Kahuna.

I stood and stared, my body broken but already mending. Whoever thought vampires were immune to pain, were wrong. We don't do flips and we aren't immune to pain. A broken bone still hurt like hell; granted, it mended faster—a lot faster.

The thing is... yeah, the thing is... learning how to better control my body seemed in my best interest. Seemed like a damned good idea, in fact. Had I been better able to control my body, I would have at least spared myself some of the hard falls I'd taken.

*Sure,* I thought. *I'll just add tumbling classes to my To-Do List.*

I was being facetious... but I really, really should add acrobatics to my repertoire. Maybe parkour, like Rand did. And being what I am, I needn't worry too much about permanently hurting myself in the process. In the least, I could save myself some pain later, especially if I faced any more demons, which I thoroughly expected to do.

"That was unreal," called a voice down the hallway.

Ah, the young artist who had created the tormented paintings. In the heat of the fight, I had almost forgotten about him. *Almost.*

I touched my shoulder and cringed. The bone

was broken in two places, maybe more, one of which was poking up through the skin. "Real enough."

The young man came toward me down the hallway, glancing in doorways as he came closer. He paused at the entrance into the living room, looked over the damaged corner and the seared claw marks along the wooden floor. I hid my damaged shoulder under my palm.

"That obvious?"

He nodded, his face wan and sickly. But I didn't think it was white from shock. I thought it was ghost-pale because this demon had the kid holed up inside the house for quite some time, painting macabre scenes like a fiend, in every sense of the word. No, if anything, the kid looked like he'd recently awakened from a nightmare.

"Did that really just happen?"

"Me killing a demon?"

"Yes."

"No," I said. "It didn't happen."

"Bullshit. I watched the whole thing. I might have been out of it, but I wasn't that out of it."

"How out of it were you?"

"It's, um... I might need a few minutes. I just sort of..."

"Got out of a dark enchantment?"

"Yes."

"Take your time."

"Your shoulder is broken. Wait, it's your

collarbone. Or both. I can take a look at it. I went to EMT school."

"But didn't graduate?"

He came over to me. "What can I say? I listened to the muse."

"You dropped out to be a painter."

His hands moved toward my shoulder and paused. "I was always a painter. I just decided to start making a living at it. Seemed a better choice than the alternative."

"Working for the Man?"

"Something like that. You must be in awful pain."

"I was, but it's healing now."

"Healing?"

"Yes."

"Can I have a closer look?"

"Knock yourself out."

He did so, tentatively touching the bone that was poking outside of my collar. Most importantly, it was poking outside of my skin too.

"Do you realize you have a compound fracture?"

"I do, yes."

"Oh, shit!"

"What?"

"The bones just... moved. Wait... they're aligning and retracting, slowly, back inside your skin. Skin is smoothing over. Healing fast. Am I still dreaming?"

"No."

I gave him a small prompt to calm down and to accept that I quickly healed, that all was well with me, and that the demonic fog that was still hanging over him, which I had to push through, was clearing rapidly.

"My name is Sam. I'm here to help. Tell me about the demon," I said.

He did. He had moved in about five months ago, and all was well. His paintings were selling more and more and he'd just landed a contract with an ebook publisher to produce original paintings for their books. Who knew ebooks could sell so well? He certainly didn't, and he wasn't complaining, the pay was good... and most importantly, it was steady. All was well with his creative work until three months ago.

"What happened three months ago?"

"I bought that."

I followed his pointing finger. Even for a room filled with the horrific, one painting stood out from the rest. It featured a grinning man with a snake going through his ears, eyes and mouth. Blood poured from all orifices. In the background were burning hills and burning cave openings. Twisted figures writhed in the flames. And rising behind it all, looming, was a horned demon with red eyes. Okay, I hadn't seen the horned types yet, but, yeah, that painting was creepy as hell.

"What made you buy that painting?"

"It, um... called to me."

He told me more. It was at an estate sale where the previous owner had burned to death in a house fire centered in and around only the kitchen. Much of the house survived, including this painting. He couldn't take his eyes off the bloody piece. He hated it instantly, but felt himself drawn to it nonetheless. With buyers swarming all around, he was lost in the painting. He was certain, yes, he was certain he could see the fire crackling. And was that a distant scream he heard? What was happening?

And then he heard the voice.

In particular, he heard his name being called. *Garrett.*

"It was a whisper at first," he said to me now, as we sat together on his couch. The sun was damn close to setting and I was getting jittery. I caught my knee bouncing, stopped it, caught it again then just let the damn thing bounce. "But then the voice got louder and louder, and I was certain I was losing my mind."

"So you did the obvious thing... you turned and ran."

"Trust me, a thousand times over, I wish I'd turned and run."

"But you didn't."

"No."

"Why not?"

"I was... fascinated. I was horrified. I was electrified. It was a painting that talked to me, for chrissakes. I was certain that something greater was happening. You see, I'd wished for so long for greater success... I don't know. I just saw the painting as an answer to my prayers."

"Paintings with people burning in them are rarely answers to prayers."

"I know... it's just that..."

"You were willing to do anything for success."

"Yes, Sam. Anything."

"Even to buy a demonic painting against your better judgment."

He ran his fingers through his hair. "I can't look at it anymore."

"You won't have to."

"You will take it, then?" He shot me both a relieved and horrified look. Indeed, within his aura, something black and oily roiled and coiled... but it was faint. I suspected, with the demon in the house, it had been thicker and more prominent. But there was still an attachment to it. The painting *had* him, and if it wasn't this demon, it would be another.

"Yes."

"I... I don't know what to say... or think."

The painting wasn't just any painting. And neither were the hellish paintings scattered throughout the house. They seemed... real. As if, yes, as if they were depicting real scenes of hell.

"What happened after you returned home with the painting?" I asked.

He told me. Almost immediately, his own work

shifted. Darker and darker, bloodier and bloodier. He painted like a man possessed, which he undoubtedly was. He painted into all hours of the night, and, at one point, he painted for three straight days, until he collapsed. When he ran out of red paint, he often used his own blood, bleeding onto his palette. Worse, he *liked* using his own blood. He liked cutting himself.

The blood, I suspected, had been a sacrifice of sorts. Or a feeding frenzy for the demon. That I required the same sustenance was too depressing to contemplate for too long, so I encouraged him to continue his tale.

"My world was turned upside down. I lost contact with friends and family and clients. I lost whole weeks, Sam. Months bled into the next. Literally. I lost all sense of who I was and what I was doing. But still I... had to create more and more..."

I didn't tell him what I thought. I didn't tell him that he was, undoubtedly, a creator, and his skills were being used to either create a world of nightmare, or to bring this world of nightmare here to earth. Perhaps a little of both.

"Okay, bud. We have work to do."
"What kind of work?"
"Do you have a machete?"
"No."
"Big knives?"
"Pretty big."

"Good enough."

## 26.

It was a lot of work to destroy his demon-inspired art, but we did it.

With my broken collarbone and shoulder well on the way back to normal, thanks to my vampire powers, we sliced and shredded and tore, and slashed through it all in a frenzy of destructive activity. Still, I wondered if we were doing any good. I had met another such creator, a writer. If Charlie Reed, say, destroyed the pages of his manuscript... did that mean the World of Dur was destroyed, too? Or parts of it? And what if some version of the story lived on as a backup, or in the cloud, whatever the hell that is? And, of course, what if it had gone to print and many thousand copies of it existed worldwide? Hell, I had a copy of it in my email somewhere and so did Allison. I remembered sneakily emailing it to us. Would all versions have to be destroyed? Or, as a creator, if his *intention* was to destroy part of his world... would that be enough?

The thing is... I suspected so, which was why I let Garrett have a hand in all of the paintings' destruction as well. So I made sure his intent was clear before destroying any of the paintings. At first, he had been reluctant to harm his paintings... until I pointed out that a) they sucked, and b) he hadn't really painted them from a good place inside of him, and c) his feelings and artwork were the after-effects and products of having been demon-possessed for the past few months.

"Was I really demon-possessed?" he asked.

"How long has it been since you changed your shirt?"

"I don't know."

"How long since you called your parents?"

"My dad is dead."

"Since you called your mom. And I'm sorry to hear that."

"A few weeks."

"Weeks?"

"Okay, months."

"Do you have much memory at all of the last few months?"

"Just painting like a crazy person."

"Or a possessed person. When did you shower last?"

"I smell that bad?"

"Worse."

He nodded. And so we cut and hacked, and basically made a mess of the place, all while Garrett came more and more to his senses. "I loved painting those paintings. It felt good painting them. I felt alive. I felt like I was a part of something big. But also..."

I had just stuck a heavy-duty steak knife through the heart of a painting that I was sure was something no one, nowhere, ever wanted to meet, in this world, or the next or anywhere. The thing dripped evil, and it was bad to the bone. I could almost, almost hear it cry out. I cut it again and again, until only remnants of its red eyes, long hair, long nails, and long face remained. A jigsaw puzzle from hell, truly.

"Go on," I said.

"I was scared, too." He looked up from his own cutting. "I was afraid... all of the time. I sensed I was creating something bigger than me, something important. But I also knew... yeah, I also knew something bad was happening, too. I was painting something that should not exist, that didn't belong in this world. In particular, I was painting a man, over and over."

"Which man?"

"Hold on."

He got up and disappeared down the hallway, then came back a few seconds later lugging a dozen or so more paintings he'd had stashed in the backroom. He set them before me, and each depicted the same tall man in a black suit. He was bald and had slits for eyes, and long, long fingers... fingers that ended in curved nails. Blood dripped from the slits in his eyes in each of the paintings.

I swallowed. "Any idea who he is?"

"Yes, Sam. I was told who he was, and I was told he would come for his paintings."

"Did he come?"

"Yes. He took some of them, not all."

"How long ago was this?"

"Maybe a few days ago. Maybe a few weeks ago. I've lost all track of time."

"Fine. Who is this man?"

Except as soon as I asked the question, I knew the answer. I didn't have to read the kid's mind to do so, either. I merely had to look at the face in the paintings. No, I didn't recognize it, but I recognized the evil.

"He said he was the devil. The new devil, whatever that means."

The bastard was back—or a version of him. This shouldn't have surprised me. There was just too much belief in him. Too much fear of him, too. The good news is... and I hoped it was good news... was that the devil might just put a kink in the dark master's plans. Then again, I also knew this to be a new iteration of the devil. A new version. A new everything. Did he step into the mindset of the past devil, basically picking up where his predecessor left off? Or did he come in fresh, with his own ideas, his own plans, learning as he went along? I suspected the latter.

"Sam, what are you?"

"I'm just a mom."

"I saw you take on that demon. I watched it all."

I dipped into his mind and gave him a suggestion to get off the subject of me, and to focus on destroying the last of these evil-ass paintings. I was pleased to see his mind was, in fact, clearing. It seemed with each painting destroyed, the hold on him was less and less. Indeed, even the slinking blackness coiling through his aura had diminished to just a thread. The blackness, I suspected, might always be there, although the demon was long gone. Once you opened a doorway to the devil, it was always open. In the least, he would always be susceptible to later possession. I might want to follow up with this one.

While I was in there, I gave him a few more suggestions. I instructed him to burn all the remaining paintings... every bit of them. I gave a delayed command, too, something I'd only recently realized I could do. I suggested to him that once he was done burning the paintings that he would have no memory of the devil or demons or of his possession. He would have no memory of me either. The command would go into effect when the last of his paintings were gone... and after he had showered for an hour.

Yes, an hour.

When we were done slicing and dicing, and I was confident I'd done my best to clean up this mess—all the while wondering just how many of the evil bastards had escaped from the paintings and lived on in this world—I spotted a breath of fresh air in the kitchen.

It was a painting in the window over the sink that was being used to cover a broken window. The painting was... unlike anything I'd ever seen before. Lovely, and beautiful, full of rich, bold colors, thick and heavy and confident brushstrokes. Clearly impressionistic, and obviously inspired by Van Gogh himself. Except this painting was... dreamlike and surreal, wild and imaginative. On second thought, it was not so different from Van Gogh's own "Starry Night." Except this scene played out across a wheat field. A purple wheat field, mind you. The sky was orange and dotted with red stars. Distant cows were pink... and not really cows, either. They were slimmer, smaller, hornier. Well, three horns. Something that might have been a farmhouse with a smoking chimney was off in the distance. Except this house was a solitary tower. Most prominent were the two figures in the field, walking together, hand-in-hand. One was older, taller, gaunt. One was smaller, younger. Both seemed lost in conversation... except, there wasn't a lot of detail on the faces. One was clearly a woman, one was a man. Were they lovers? I didn't know, but that wasn't the impression I got.

*Friends,* I thought.

"You like the painting?" asked Garrett behind me.

"I do. A lot."

"It came with the house. I found it in the attic."

"And you decided to cover a broken window with it?"

"Well, it's not exactly my style. A little too derivative, if you ask me. I gravitate towards originality."

With my back to him, he hadn't seen me roll my eyes, but I did. "But you liked it enough to bring it down here."

"It's not a bad painting. Lightens up the place."

I laughed at that, and so did he. After all, his delayed memory command hadn't gone into effect just yet. "I'm sure your demon wasn't too happy about it."

"Well, we rarely went into the kitchen. You might be surprised to learn that I had weighed close to three hundred pounds."

I spun, gasping. "Have you eaten these past few months?"

He shrugged. "I remember going through every last bit of food in my house, but eventually, I ran out. I remember one morning eating my toothpaste."

"You need a bacon burger. Stat!"

"Tell me about it."

"But first, the paintings," I cautioned.

He nodded. "Yes, the paintings, of course. I should burn them."

"What a good idea."

"Say, do you want this painting as a sort of thank you for, you know, plugging up whatever gateway to hell I'd opened?"

He hadn't opened a gateway to hell. He had created whole worlds. Or one whole world. One horrific, terrible world full of nightmare. Then again, what did I know? And the idea of owning this painting gripped me and wouldn't let go. Yes, I *had* to have this painting. I just had to. No doubt about it.

Wait, wasn't that exactly what Garrett had thought when he had seen the hideous painting at the estate sale (which we had long since cut to smithereens). It was. But this was different. This painting wasn't... evil. At least, I didn't think it was.

"Are you sure?" I asked. I could feel my heartbeat increasing, which said a lot.

"Oh, yes—ha! You are fast."

I had, after all, already snatched it from its perch above the sink. "Thank you," I said.

"Hey, it's not for everybody. Glad you liked it. And thank you again," he said, "for all your help. I'm not sure what would have happened to me in here if you hadn't come along."

"I suspect you might have started eating the furniture."

"Or my own arm. Sam, did those paintings come to life?"

"They might have."

"How?"

"It's a long story, and you're going to forget all about it."

"I will?"

"Yes, just like you are going to forget this conversation in a few seconds."

"I will? What are you talking—hey, thank you again for all your help..."

"We covered that part already," I said. I was about to leave with my new painting, which was just small enough for me to carry under my arm, so I did so, carefully. Suddenly, this painting was my new favorite thing. The thing was... Garrett was a creator. A powerful one, and I instructed him to contact me should any nefarious types want to use his skills again, and he understood, and permanently memorized my phone number with my help. Next, I told him to paint what was in his heart, to enjoy it, to love it, to live it, and he nodded.

And so I left. One demon down.

Except the devil was back.

A *different* devil, whatever the hell that meant. Let's just hope that *this* devil stayed away from Sam Moon... and her Devil Killer.

At least I had my painting.

## 27.

The library was popping.

The business of education was alive and well at the campus of Cal State Fullerton, located in Fullerton, California, sandwiched between a busy freeway on one side and a busy boulevard on the other. Residential houses, doctors' offices, and shopping centers crowded for space amid the dozens of fraternity and sorority houses. It was a lively place, even if the students seemed to be getting younger and younger. Or I was getting older and older, although you couldn't tell. Allison tells me that I could pass for a twenty-five-year-old, but I doubted it, since I could still see myself with full makeup on, and I still looked thirtyish to me, no matter what. Thirty was a good age. Not too young, not too old. If the conspiring dark masters had done me any service, it was to turn me at the prime of my life, unlike my one-time father, Jeffcock, who'd been turned much later in life.

So there was a chance I might have actually fit in with the swarming crowds of students flooding in and out of the many entrances into the many building. I was surprised to see a new Starbucks in the library. Yes, a Starbucks *inside a library*. Like the old Jay Leno joke goes, "Someday, Starbucks will open a Starbucks inside a Starbucks."

I was tempted to order a breve latte on my way to see the Alchemist, but decided against it. Coffee and dangerous occult books didn't seem to mix. Then again, a coffee cup sporting a cryptic two-tailed mermaid on the logo seemed to go hand-in-hand with a secret occult reading room.

Okay, I talked myself into it.

A few minutes later, with my iced breve latte in hand, I stepped inside the elevator and punched the button for the third floor.

\*\*\*

The door into the Occult Reading Room is obvious to my eyes; not so obvious to the eyes of others. In fact, it's downright invisible.

I was never sure how the Alchemist managed to pull off that trick, but I suspected it had to do with his own great telepathic abilities, rivaled only by my own daughter, and maybe the bitch inside me, too. Max, I suspected, could read the thoughts of any and all who sought the Occult Reading Room... or those he deemed worthy of finding it. He knew their intentions, and he and he alone decided who was given access. I suspected the door was always there, but a simple spell kept it hidden. When a person was deemed worthy, the spell, and its illusion, was removed temporarily for them.

Call it a working theory.

"And a very good theory at that," said a voice from down the hallway, followed by the young-looking Alchemist himself. His hands were clasped behind his back. He wore gray slacks and a black shirt. "But consider how few actually know about the room."

"I knew about it."

"You were told about it."

He was right, of course. Fang had known about it. Then again, Fang knew about everything. Still, Fang hadn't known exactly how to find the room, and, to my knowledge, still hadn't set foot in it. Which didn't much matter. I had seen Fang's own occult library and it was considerable. Not quite as extensive as the Alchemist's, but damn close to it.

I found myself thinking back to my first introduction to the Occult Reading Room—and to the Alchemist, aka, the Librarian, himself. "A young man at the help desk told me about the Occult Reading Room," I said. "He seemed confused at first, then told me where to find it—wait, no way!

You were the young man?"

"Not quite, Sam. But I did influence his mind and words, and gave him the information you needed."

"He was super flirty, if I recall."

"And so were you, Sam."

"Geez, you're everywhere," I said.

"It may seem that way. But here, in the library, I'm where I need to be to give access to those who need it."

That seemed smart and clever, and more magical than I could wrap my brain around. Which lent itself to a question I had been thinking since reading my sire's/father's account. "What's the difference between an alchemist and a witch?"

"One, you're born with, the other, you cultivate through years of practice. Decades of practice. Hell, I'm still practicing it."

I thought of my one-time father's story. Although a vampire, he'd cultivated the basics of magic.

"He cultivated the basics of alchemy, I would suggest," said Max. "And he became quite good at it, I see. Sam, would you mind terribly if I reviewed the letter?"

"I don't have it with me."

He pointed to my head. "It's all up there. Every word."

"But I don't remember every word."

"Your subconscious does."

I shrugged. "Knock yourself out."

"Thank you."

I spent fifteen, twenty minutes perusing the row of dark and dangerous books, ignoring the pleading calls of the entities trapped within, many of whom called out to the entity within me. Lots of trapped souls around here. I knew now that Elizabeth had been the one-time owner of these books. Who and what entities were trapped within, I didn't want to know. For her part, Elizabeth seemed uninterested in their plight, ignoring their pleas for help and escape, even while she herself remained quiet, deep within my own mind.

"Finished, Sam."

"You do know you're a big snoop, right?"

"So says the woman who follows people for a living."

"Touché."

"How are you feeling?" he asked me.

"You know how I'm feeling."

"I can see the different moods flowing through you. But what mood have you settled on?"

I thought about that, turning away from a small, thick book that, I was certain, was pulsating. Or throbbing. Or beating. Like a heart.

"Beating is accurate. The book is called *The Heart of Asmoor*."

"Should I ask?"

"A dark wizard—a rival, really—bound by my dear mother. All his arcane knowledge is contained in that single book."

"Along with his heart?" I said.

"It is all that is left of him, I'm afraid. Stored in a compartment at the back of the book."

"Of course it is," I said. "Because Elizabeth is creepy like that."

"She is also clever like that, too. She systemically destroyed her enemies. Worse, she bound many of them forever."

"Any particular reason why?"

"Some entities cannot be destroyed. Some just bound. Truth is, I have done my share of binding as well. Many in this room are here because of my hand."

"Like mother, like son?"

"Hardly. She did it out of revenge; I did it to preserve the peace."

"Well, you're doing a helluva good job, Max," I said, and meant it. "Last I checked, she lost a major battle."

He nodded humbly, sadly.

"Were you a major part of it?" I asked.

"Yes and no. I was young when it started, and I could not defeat the strongest of their kind. But I grew more knowledgeable as the war raged on... and found myself more on the front lines, you could say. But that is neither here nor now. At present, we need to address the entity that has, seemingly, evaded all of us for many centuries. An entity that is still killing young witches and mages the world over."

"Mages?"

"Warlocks, Sam."

"Like Harry Potter?"

"If that helps."

"It does, thank you."

Of course, I happened to know, perhaps better than most and, undoubtedly—to the delight of millions, if not billions, of fans everywhere—that the world of Harry Potter was real, that J.K. Rowling was herself a creator. Now, if I could just find a portal into *that* world, much like I did into the World of Dur last year. Hmm. Perhaps I should go look for Platform 9¾ at King's Cross Station in London...

Like, seriously.

"You can't be serious, Sam."

"Do you doubt that the world of Harry Potter is real?"

"Not for a second."

"Then somewhere there's a portal into it."

"Sam—"

"Or maybe she can just write me into the story."

"Sam—"

"Of course, I could always influence her to write me into the story..."

"Are you quite done?"

"Can I just have this moment?" I asked. "I'm picturing myself now at Hogwarts. Maybe they need a new dark arts teacher. In fact, I'm damn certain they do. Well, they did at the end of every book, like ever. Didn't she publish a play or something?"

"I haven't the faintest..."

"Never mind that. I can picture it now. Picture *me* now..."

"I know you can. Oh, wow. My eyes."

I laughed.

"Who's Remus Lupin?" asked Max. "Oh, I see, he's the werewolf."

"What can I say? I have a type."

"Can we move on?"

"Wait... hold on. Score!"

"Were you just playing..."

"Yes," I said. "Quidditch."

"Are we quite done here?"

"Quite."

"And you won't compel J.K. Rowling to write you into the book?"

I shrugged. "No promises. But I don't think she's writing any more books. Or..."

"No, Sam. You will not influence her to write more books."

"Maybe just one more?"

"Starring you?"

"No, silly. Starring Harry Potter. But he and I could save the day together."

"I think we have more pressing matters, Sam."

I had one last fleeting image of me downing some butterbeer, then nodded. "The Red Rider," I said.

Max nodded. The color of his eyes sometimes varied, I imagined, due to some alchemy mystery. Today, his bright-blue eyes twinkled with something other than ambient light. There wasn't necessarily a flame in those eyes, but there was something else, something I just might have caught for the first time...

"My guardian angel, Sam. He's watching you. Through me."

"How come I never noticed it—him—before?"

"I suspect he's never been this interested before. As it turns out, you—and your one-time father, Jeffcock—aren't the only ones looking for the Red Rider."

"You're telling me this creep eludes even angels?"

"It appears so, Sam. As best as anyone knows, he has mastered the frequencies."

"Say again?"

"He can traverse through dimensions, going higher than even the angels can, if need be."

"And these words make sense to you?"

"Yes and no. Rarely does darkness travel up through the frequencies. In fact, never. Much of the spirit world is taking an interest in this case."

"It's not really a case... okay, maybe it is." The truth is, my one-time father kinda sorta did hand this one off to me. I mean, if he knew me at all, he had to know I would take it on...

"Sam, there is more than one guardian angel with us here now. They've been assembling over the past few minutes."

"Um, 'scuse me?"

"There are dozens of such beings here, with more still coming. Look again. They will briefly manifest for you."

I did look, giving it my best Clint Eastwood squint. And there they were. Dozens of them, standing before me in a semi-circle, and all looking far bigger than any mere mortal... although still not quite as big as Kingsley. My eyes naturally see into the spirit world, and I can often see Ishmael, my own one-time guardian angel when others can't see him. But I can't always see angels. Not too long ago, I met two archangels and a few more warrior-angel types. These angels now weren't fully manifested, but still... they were many, and they were beautiful.

"Sure, wow. We have an audience."

"They are offering you their full support, Sam."

"They do realize that I am, you know, the enemy?"

"Only that which hides within you offers them pause for thought. They know you fought the devil himself and won. They also know you wield the Devil Killer, and have been knighted, so to speak, by the Angel of Death himself. They understand all of that and more. Mostly, they understand that you are good at what you do, and they are putting their faith in you."

"Just this morning I was doing laundry and wondering where I'd gone wrong with my son," I said. I gave the good-looking alchemist a glimpse of my meaning. And by meaning, I meant skid mark city.

"Disturbing, Sam. But your point is not lost. They understand your situation. Maybe not the situation with your son and his briefs. But they understand your limitations and strengths. They also understand you may not succeed. So far, no one has. Not even angels. In fact, your one-time father, I am being told, came the closest to this fiend, and it took him 500 years to catch mere glimpses of him."

"Exactly. 500 years. And I've only been at this vampire business for barely longer than a decade."

"Indeed, but one of the angels is stepping forward. He is telling me you have an edge."

"I like edges."

"He is saying that, in fact, you are one of the few who can claim to have been killed by the Red Rider."

"Yeah, so. There's probably dozens, if not hundreds, of such people on the earth."

"Not as many as you would think. But that is neither here nor there. The key here is that you have been *reminded* of your murder, in vivid detail, by your one-time father."

"So? Couldn't any one of these angels do the same?"

The Alchemist gave me a sad smile. "There are limitations to an angel's interaction with his or her charge. You know that better than most, perhaps. In short, they are forbidden to divulge such information, if any. And not just forbidden. Completely incapable. Look at the lengths your own guardian angel went to just to reveal himself to you. No, Sam. You are that rare breed of both victim *and* immortal. On top of that, you are an investigator at heart. Even better, you have some powerful allies."

I did. Together, Allison, Kingsley and I could move mountains. Throw in my son and my daughter and, yeah, we were quite the little army.

"And don't forget the Devil Killer and the angels, Sam. So many angels ready to help."

"I'm still at a loss for what they think I can do that they can't. And what, exactly, do they want me to do?"

"One moment, Sam."

I nodded and squinted again at the light beings standing around the room. For some reason, they had chosen not to reveal themselves in all their glory. I suspect if they did, I might just go blind. At least temporarily.

"Sam, I'm being told they do not have the authority to tell you what to do with the Red Rider, should he be caught. I am told that you should consult with the archangel Azrael."

The Angel of Death. Sure, okay. "Why are they here, Max? The angels, I mean."

"They are lost, Sam. Their charges were stolen from them, and they could do nothing about it."

"How is the Red Rider able to do this? How is he able to steal children from under their guardian angels' noses?"

"The angels do not know. But enough is enough. They need help." Max paused and held up a finger, cocking his head to one side, listening. "They have been waiting a long time for one like you."

"How did they know any of this? I mean, I didn't even know until this morning." I snapped my fingers. "The scroll. You just read it."

"I did, and in turn, so did my guardian angel. It is safe to say that your letter sent shockwaves through the angelic world, if I may call it that. They are of one mind, as you know. And with your own guardian angel long since unattached, this information was not known until now."

"So what now?"

"That is up to you, Sam. But I am being told that another child has recently been abducted, a girl up the coast from here, in a city called Santa Barbara. A child who was quite gifted in the magical arts. She is gone now, as of a few days ago. Her angel is here with us. Through me, he will walk you through what he knows, if you are willing."

"Is this really happening?" I asked. "Are angels really asking me for help?"

"It is happening, Sam. And they are. More

children and young ones will disappear in the months and years and centuries to come, unless this bastard can be stopped."

I took in some worthless air. "This isn't exactly how I imagined our conversation would go today."

"Me either, Sam."

"I still don't know how anyone, angel or otherwise, can expect me to find this thing where others have failed."

"One moment, my friend."

I nodded, drumming my fingers over the help desk. I'm pretty sure those small indentations were from the last time I'd drummed my fingers on this very same counter. Me and my ugly-ass nails. Still, they were kinda handy sometimes. These were from Elizabeth, I had no doubt. Some of my skills and talents were from my own fully-contained soul. Others—the darker aspects—were all Elizabeth.

"Sam, although the connection is faint—indeed, barely discernible—I am being told there is a link between you and the Red Rider. Your father learned much in his years chasing the Red Rider, but he never learned of this magical connection. This would be, as the kids say, brand-new information."

I opened my mouth to speak, but found no words. I was about to tell them that I had no link when Max, whose head had been cocked to one side, continued:

"I'm being told it has to do with the physical act of the consuming of flesh, blood and magic. Magiceaters, much like vampire sires—as you recently learned—remain connected to their victim."

"Except their victims die."

"But the magic never does, not really. It merely transfers, from them to him."

"So you're saying some of my old magic is still attached to him?"

"It's a part of him, actually. Sam, I'm being told that you can learn to tap into this magic. In fact, I'm being told this is how you will find the Red Rider."

"An entity that traverses through the frequencies?"

"Yes, Sam."

"Have you ever traversed through the frequencies?"

The Librarian gave me a sad smile. "Not recently. And not for very far. There is a limit to just how far a human—and even angels—can go, although I see you were given a vision once, of such frequencies and dimensions."

I had, long ago, on an island in the Pacific Northwest. It had been, well, a glorious vision.

"But merely a vision, Sam. You didn't actually traverse the frequencies. You didn't, for instance, exist in these higher dimensions. You were merely granted a glimpse of them. An important glimpse, nonetheless, for this was intended to give you a framework for how the universe and multiverse is structured."

"Whoa, that was like... years ago."

"Time and space mean little to the higher entities."

"Has anyone traversed the frequencies?" I asked.

"A good question. There are rumors of only a few—and when I say few, I am only aware of two—who have traveled the full range of dimensions."

"The full range?" I asked. "How many are there?"

"A hundred in all."

"And God is at the top?" I asked. Except I knew this. I had seen this. I had seen the vast, swirling entity that existed beyond space and time.

"Indeed. There is no vibration, dimension or frequency higher than the Origin."

"And two have traveled to him?"

"Yes."

"Is the Red Rider one of them?"

"No, but I am being told he got close."

"And the others?"

"One is a holy man in England."

"Is he still alive?"

"Sadly, no. The other is in India."

I nodded. "How high have you traveled, Max?"

"Only to the fifth dimension."

"Only? Okay. And the angels?"

"They exist in the fourth and can go no higher."

I nodded, taking this all in.

"What's the fifth dimension like?" I asked.

"Wild, Sam. But that's a discussion for another day."

"And you expect me to chase this thing through the higher dimensions? Something only two other people have done before?"

"Two known people, and yes."

"But I don't know what to do... or even where to start."

Max tilted his head to one side, seemed to be listening to something beyond my hearing, and nodded. "I'm being told that you've been given the starting place."

"I have?"

He smiled. "Think back. A clue was recently given to you."

I blinked. The only thing given to me recently was...

"The painting?" I asked.

"That would be it."

I bit my lip, and was about to protest that it was just a painting. But I had recently seen that some paintings could be more than paintings. I saw it again in my mind's eye... in particular, the two figures walking hand-in-hand in the field. The two blurred figures. Blurred, yes... but also oddly familiar, too.

The small, dark-haired woman was...

"She's me," I said.

The Alchemist only shrugged.

"And the man?" I asked.

"Think, Sam."

A name popped in my head... a name I couldn't believe, but I found myself uttering it anyway. "Van Gogh."

"That would be the one. He was, of course, a creator. Or perhaps better stated, he *is* a creator. More importantly..."

I held up a finger, suddenly sure where Max was going with this. "Let me guess: he paints the higher frequencies."

"Yes. I'm being told that Vincent painted himself into immortality. He is waiting for you."

"Waiting where..." But I stopped myself. I knew exactly where. "In the purple fields."

"That would be the place."

"Fine," I said. "But before I do anything, before I travel the frequencies, whatever the hell that means, before I meet Van Gogh, whatever the hell *that* means... first, I must find this missing little girl."

*The End*
*(of Part One)*

J.R. RAIN

*To be continued in:*
# *Moon Master*
*Vampire for Hire #16*
*(Red Rider: Part 2)*
*Coming soon!*

*About the Author:*

**J.R. Rain** is an ex-private investigator who now writes full-time. He lives in a small house on a small island with his small dog, Sadie. Please visit him at www.jrrain.com.

Printed in Great Britain
by Amazon